"Have faith in me, Ariel…"

"Why are you taking such an interest in my business?" Ariel asked.

Scott's eyes first took in the thin blue T-shirt that molded itself to her curves, then went down to her narrow waist and rounded derriere. "Oh, it's not your business I'm interested in, Ariel."

She felt her face flush at his scrutiny. "I told you—"

"I know what you told me, but I like a challenge. Tell me something else. Was your ex-husband a gentleman?"

She nodded.

"I'm not."

There was a long moment when their eyes locked, and then he reached out for her and pulled her to him, one hand around her waist and the other tipping her face up so that her lips met his.…

ABOUT THE AUTHOR

Ever popular Beverly Sommers is the author of various published short stories and novels. Beverly drew on her own experience as a one-time art-gallery owner in Southern California for the background of this book. She currently resides in New York City.

Books by Beverly Sommers

HARLEQUIN AMERICAN ROMANCE

HARLEQUIN INTRIGUE

These books may be available at your local bookseller.

Don't miss any of our special offers. Write to us at the following address for information on our newest releases.

Harlequin Reader Service
P.O. Box 52040, Phoenix, AZ 85072-2040
Canadian address: P.O. Box 2800, Postal Station A,
5170 Yonge St., Willowdale, Ont. M2N 6J3

Mix
and Match

BEVERLY SOMMERS

Harlequin Books

TORONTO • NEW YORK • LONDON
AMSTERDAM • PARIS • SYDNEY • HAMBURG
STOCKHOLM • ATHENS • TOKYO • MILAN

Published January 1985

ISBN 0-373-16085-2

Printed in Canada

Chapter One

"Shades of Rose Saunders, I do believe. I'm surprised Red Ryan would allow such subversive goings-on in his domain."

Startled by the low, amused voice behind her when she had thought she was alone in the shop, Ariel momentarily lost control of her hold on the small brush in her hand, causing her to smear the intricate still life of daisies in a pewter pitcher that she was painting. Then the words sank in, and a chuckle escaped her.

"You're quite right—he'd disown me," she admitted.

"As well he should. *Blue daisies?*"

"I also do them in pink, white, yellow and, on one notable occasion, violet."

"Somehow, I'm not surprised."

Ariel turned around on her stool, fully intending to berate whoever it was who had caused her to turn the daisy into something more nearly resembling a weed, only to have the words catch in her throat at the first glimpse of the stranger in her shop. He was stunningly attractive, even for Southern California, which is noted for its handsome men. Thick, curly blond hair framed a strongly chiseled face. The gleam in his aquamarine eyes caught her attention, but it didn't dissuade her from continuing her inspection. A bushy, blond mustache partly obscured the strong mouth; her eyes traveled down over his tan, firmly muscled chest to his narrow waist, and then on down to the strong legs emphasized by the cutoff jeans he was wearing. He was like a statue, a sculptor's ideal, refined over and over in clay before chisel was ever put to stone. Her eyes went back up to his face. He smiled, a crooked incisor marring the perfection and bringing Ariel out of her reverie.

"You ruined my painting," she managed to say at last.

"Oh, is that what you were thinking? And all along I thought you were looking me over."

Annoyed, Ariel turned back to her easel.

"And anyway," continued the voice behind her, "you can't ruin a Rose Saunders special, which is about the only good thing you can say about them."

"Another artist," she muttered, vainly trying to fix the damage she had inflicted upon the canvas.

"I'll have to plead guilty to that," he acknowledged.

"Personally, I think you're all jealous of Rose, including my father, and I've told him so. Rose is very successful. She sells everything she paints, which is more than can be said for the rest of you."

"And money is the mark of success, of course."

"You're damn right it is!"

"Well, you don't look like Red, and I wasn't even aware he had a daughter, but you sure as hell have his temper," he said, amusement in his voice.

Ariel, who considered herself very even-tempered,

shot him an annoyed glance over her shoulder. "Did you need some help?" It had only belatedly occurred to her that he might be a customer, and she could use more of them.

"No, but you do," he said enigmatically, and then, taking the brush out of her hand, repaired the damage with a few, sure strokes, something that would have taken her ten times longer to do, and even then she wouldn't have done it as well.

Dabbing the brush in the paint on her palette, he quickly painted a very lifelike daisy, down to a drop of moisture on one of its petals. His arm was by her face as he painted, a scent of sun and salt emanating from it. It was a good, clean smell, but the proximity of the scantily clad man was making her nervous. She ducked under his arm and moved some distance away from him.

"I think you took lessons from Rose," she accused him, thinking that he painted daisies every bit as well as her teacher. Her father had derided what he termed the "old ladies' school of painting," of which Rose Saunders was the leading proponent in the area. For her part, Ariel was impressed with Rose's teaching ability; she'd only been taking lessons from the woman for six months, but already she was selling everything she painted and getting commissions for more. And for the next lesson Rose had promised her class to teach them how to paint California missions, which Ariel knew would sell well.

He handed the brush back to her, seemingly bored by the easy exercise. "How do you know Rose didn't take lessons from me?"

"Because she told us she's been painting for forty

years, and you're not that old." She didn't think he was much more than thirty, although Californians looked so young sometimes it was hard to tell.

"Maybe she painted lousy for the first twenty before she came to me for help."

"But you think she still paints lousy," countered Ariel, having learned a little bit about logical arguing from her father.

He grinned. "Touché. Just keep at it and one of these days you'll be painting as well as Rose."

If anyone else had said that to her, Ariel would take it as a compliment. In this case, however...

"If you want to learn to paint, why don't you have Red teach you?" he suggested.

"He did."

She seemed to have rendered him speechless for a moment. Then, "Where is Red, anyway? Is he around?"

"You didn't hear?"

"Hear what?"

Ariel had thought the whole town knew about it. "Aren't you a friend of his?"

He shrugged. "We're drinking buddies, fellow painters...."

"He got married. A year ago."

He looked shocked at the news, his mouth dropping open, Ariel noted with surprise. "Red. *Married?* I leave the country for a year and...I just don't believe it!"

Ariel had found it pretty hard to believe herself, especially since her father's new bride was two years younger than Ariel was. Christine's share of community property from her divorce had made it possible for the newly married couple to purchase a van and travel around Mexico, a place her father had always been eager to paint.

He still looked stunned. "Poor Red. Marriage is the kiss of death for an artist."

"What?" Ariel almost laughed at his serious tone.

"You heard me. Marriage is the last thing an artist needs."

"And just what does an artist need?" she asked him, amused by how deeply affected he seemed to be by her father's marriage. She didn't agree with him in the least. Her father's most productive years had been when her mother was alive. On the other hand, for a woman artist it probably was the kiss of death. She was painting much more prolifically since her own divorce.

"What does an artist need? Variety, a certain restlessness, a sense of insecurity. An artist needs to be a free spirit."

All of which sounded just like her father during the past ten years, despite the fact that when her mother had been around, he'd been waited on hand and foot. *How soon they forget,* she mused.

"When's he coming back?" he asked her.

"Dad? Not for another year."

"That's a pretty long honeymoon."

"Christine's treating him to two years of painting in Mexico, all expenses paid."

He gave a low whistle of admiration, then got up and began walking around the back of the shop. He stopped to look at the folding easels stacked in one corner, a reminder of the painting class Red had started to teach in the back room and then aborted because he couldn't stand the mediocre and downright poor caliber of his students. He walked around the fitting table, complete with tools, and then bent down and surveyed the stack of glass and mat board Ariel had recently purchased.

"Well, he's got the most important thing, at least," he murmured.

"What?" For some reason Ariel wasn't following his train of thought.

"Time. That's primarily what an artist needs. For most people time is money, but for artists it's the other way around. For us money is time—time to paint. And it's damn hard to get enough of it. I'm glad for him; I think this is just what he needed. We used to get into a lot of arguments about art, your dad and me, and what it always boiled down to was I thought he was getting too damn commercial."

He made commercial sound like a dirty word. "Well, maybe you're able to starve for the sake of pure art, but for me time is money. I've got two daughters to support, and I'm going to put out these pretty little pictures just as fast as I can."

His mustache seemed to twitch with amusement. "Enter the inestimable Rose Saunders...."

Ariel flashed him a warning look. "Let's not get into an argument about Rose. She's a very nice, very talented lady."

He raised his hands in surrender. "I promise to treat her with the same respect I treat my own mother. Why not? They both paint about the same."

He was leaning against the fitting table, his long, muscular legs crossed in front of him, the hair on them bleached white by the sun. He reached into the pocket of his cutoffs and took out a crushed pack of cigarettes, removing one and lighting it. He surveyed her slowly through the smoke. "You sure don't look like Red."

She nodded in agreement, knowing she bore no resemblance to the red-haired giant who was her father. She took after her mother, who had been petite and dark with a gamine look, a throwback to her French ancestry. She had also inherited her mother's curves, and she glanced down, glad that the painting smock she was wearing disguised them from the stranger's probing eyes.

He seemed to sense that his inspection was unnerving her and looked toward the front of the shop. "I see Red put in a line of custom framing."

That had been Ariel's innovation. Her father had used the shop more or less as a studio in which to paint and as a meeting place for other artists. The occasional sale of one of his paintings had paid the rent on the store and the tiny apartment above it, and he wouldn't have wanted to bother with the business details involved in framing. When Ariel had made the decision to quit her job and take over the running of the shop, she had contacted Windflower, a local framing factory, which supplied her with corner samples of all their custom framing. They had also taught her to cut glass and mat boards and fit the pictures so that she could take care of that part of the framing herself and thus make all the profits.

"I put that in," she told him. "I needed something to make the shop pay. Only so far it hasn't worked that well, since hardly anyone knows I have it."

"Where are you advertising?"

"I'm not."

"Why not?"

"I can't afford it," said Ariel, wishing he wouldn't ask so many probing questions.

"You can't afford not to. Why don't you ask Red for the money? I bet he'd think it was a good idea."

"It's not his concern anymore. He gave me the shop when he left. Actually, he told me to get rid of it, but I wanted to see if I could make it a success. I liked the idea of having my own business." She didn't know why she was revealing so much to a perfect stranger, someone she'd never seen before today. It was kind of nice, though, to have someone to talk business with.

"You could at least put a sign in your window."

Ariel sighed. She should have thought of that herself. Maybe she had been wrong and she didn't have the proper kind of mind to run a business. Her husband had told her that often enough, generally when she failed to balance their checking account properly. Well, it wasn't too late. She could make a sign right now and stick it in the window, and maybe the stranger would tell his friends she did custom framing, and the word would get around.

Ariel reached into a box filled with scraps of mat boards and pulled out a piece about five by seven inches, then found a felt-tip pen and began to print CUSTOM FRAMING in large letters.

"You've got to think big," she heard him say. She found herself watching him in alarm as he removed a new piece of expensive mat board from its carton, then rummaging around her paintbox until he found her largest brush. "Get me some black paint," he ordered.

"But that's a new piece of board," she protested.

"Listen, we're talking advertising. You need a large sign—something people can see as they drive by."

She decided not to pursue the argument since his use of logic seemed every bit as good as hers, and instead she squeezed out a large glob of black paint onto her palette for him.

She stood by wordlessly and watched as a beautifully painted sign began to emerge from his brushwork. It looked professional and announced in large letters that the Sandpiper Gallery—her own innovation, Red hadn't even had a name for the shop—was now in the business of custom framing and also gave a twenty percent discount to artists.

"A twenty percent discount?" she asked.

"You've got to have some inducement," he told her, "otherwise we'd just deal directly with the frame factories. Most of the factories give artists with resale numbers a fifteen percent discount."

He finished the sign, then stood back from it to admire his work. "What do you think?"

"Are you a sign painter?"

He laughed. "Hardly."

"You should be. You're very good."

"I'm afraid painting signs wouldn't satisfy my soul."

"It would probably be good money, though."

"You lack the soul of an artist, daughter of Red. What is your name, anyway? I'm Scott. Scott Campbell."

"Ariel," she told him, automatically holding out her hand. He didn't seem eager to release it despite the tugging from her end.

"That's very pretty. It suits you, too; there's something about you that suggests a water sprite, even though you don't look like you've been out in the sun much. Don't you ever get to the beach?"

Although the shop was only two blocks from the ocean, she rarely saw the beach; she kept the shop open six days a week and then went out on art shows on Sundays. "I haven't had time," she told him matter-of-factly, not knowing quite how to deal with his teasing, flirtatious manner. Good heavens, didn't he know how old she was? Or did he come on to all women, regardless of age?

Scott dropped her hand and picked up the sign. "Come on, let's fix up your window."

She followed him to the front of the shop, where he removed one of her daisy paintings that was propped up in a small display easel in the window, substituting the sign instead. She looked around the gallery, trying to see it the way a customer would. Once it had been filled with Red's outrageously colorful paintings; now there were only a few of her own scattered around on the walls, making the shop look empty and forlorn. She had to admit that there was hardly enough to attract customers even when they did come in, even though she was painting them as fast as she could. It was a good thing she had decided to put in the custom framing; at least it would give her something customers might want.

"Bring me some of those corner samples," Scott called to her.

She went over to the wall where she hung the framing samples and took down a few. She chose some in wood, some in primary colors with mylar strips, and a few with colorful burlap liners. She handed them to Scott, and he arranged them quickly and artistically around the sign in a way she never would have thought of. Then he went out the door of the shop, beckoning for her to follow.

Once she was on the sidewalk, she had to admit the

sign was an eye-catcher. The only thing marring her new window display was a battered bicycle leaning against the plate glass. In a town where many of the adults rode sleek, ten-speed racers, this bicycle looked like an anachronism. The original paint was obscured by rust, the leather seat was worn and tattered, and an ugly wooden box was affixed to its rear fender.

Scott laughed at her expression of distaste. "Don't ever play poker," he warned her. "Your face gives everything away. The bike's mine. It doesn't look like much, but it gets me around, and it hasn't been stolen once."

She could believe that—who would want to steal it?

"I take it you don't have a bike."

She shook her head. "No."

"Well, it's big business around here stealing ten-speeds. The thieves go around in vans and just lift them off the street, locked or not. I like riding a bike, but I don't want to be constantly having to look out for it."

Ariel nodded, having heard about such bike thieves from her daughters. And judging by his appearance and taking into account that he was an artist, he probably couldn't afford to have his only means of transportation stolen.

He lifted up the lid of the wooden box and removed a black portfolio. "Now that you're in business, I just happen to need some custom framing," he told her with a wink.

"You don't have to feel obligated," she began to protest, but he raised his hand to silence her.

"I don't feel obligated," he assured her, "but your twenty percent discount saves me a long bike ride to the frame factory.'' He headed into the shop. ''Just one thing—I'll need them by Saturday.''

Ariel thought quickly. It was Wednesday, but if she called the order in before five she could get them in Friday's delivery. ''I can have them for you then,'' she told him.

''I'll need them fitted.''

''I can do that Friday night.''

''I've got quite a few.''

''How many?''

He put down the portfolio on the table she had positioned in front of the framing samples on the wall. She took her place behind the table, nervously straightening the samples of mat board that were displayed on a stand on the table.

He took out a stack of signed and numbered lithographs. ''I'd say a couple of dozen.''

''I thought you painted,'' she said, surprised by the prints.

''I do. I also do an occasional suite, mostly for my own entertainment.''

''Suite?''

''A series on one subject. In the manner of Picasso or Dali.''

She nodded, remembering having heard of them.

He turned the pictures around and spread some of them out for her inspection. They were like nothing she had ever seen. In black and white, they were grotesque caricatures of men: evil generals with long, drooping mustaches, lascivious-looking revolutionaries in combat fatigues, cigarettes hanging from the corners of their slack mouths. It wasn't a contrast of good and evil—they all looked evil—and yet at the same time there was a distinct humor to them. Ariel knew her younger daughter would be crazy about them.

"What do you think?" he asked her.

She hesitated. "I don't know. You're very talented, but I just don't know. Is there a name for the group?"

"I'm calling it *Banana Republic.*"

She laughed. "Yes, I do like them. They're rather like political cartoons."

"Another thing your father and I argued about. He doesn't think art and politics mix. Like Daumier with his suites of doctors and lawyers, I like to make a social comment now and then."

"Rose would disagree with you, too," said Ariel, making him laugh.

"Do you disagree with me?"

She thought about it a moment, then remembered her reaction when she had seen Picasso's *Guernica* for the first time. "No, I think you're right. I like paintings that say something, that aren't just pretty."

"Despite the fact that you don't paint them yourself."

"I told you, I paint for money."

He was looking through the mat samples, pulling out the ones in textured ivory and off-white. Then he took a chrome corner sample off the wall and placed it over one of the mat samples. "Do you have any silver mat board?"

She nodded and found the sample for him.

"Here's what I want: double mats, a thin lip of silver and two inches of ivory. Chrome framing and regular glass."

Ariel, who felt as though he was doing her job for her, suggested nonglare glass.

He grinned at her. "Trying to run the price up?"

"No. I just like the looks of it."

"You can't use nonglare with a double mat—you get a distortion," he informed her.

She felt stupid for having suggested it but nonetheless was glad of the information. She still had a lot to learn about the business.

"Are you sure you can fit all these by Saturday morning?"

Ariel figured the only way she could fit two dozen pictures would be to stay up all night on Friday doing it, but she didn't mind, considering the amount of business he was giving her. "I think so," she murmured, hoping he wouldn't change his mind and go elsewhere.

"I'll come by and help you with them."

She thought about working side by side with him on Friday night and didn't think it was a very good idea. There was something about him that made her nervous, and she didn't want to botch the job of fitting the pictures. "Maybe you could stop by and see that I do the first one right, and then I can do the rest on my own."

"We'll see," Scott said in much the same tone of voice she used with her children, and then began to measure his pictures with a yardstick, writing down figures on the pad she kept at the table for such purposes. She noted that he was much quicker with fractions than she was.

When he was finished he handed her the measurements for the frames, and she filled out a work order. Then she excused herself to call in the order from the back room. She thought he might possibly leave while she was on the phone, but when she returned he was still there, looking around at her paintings.

"Thank you very much for the order, Scott, and for all your help. I really appreciate it."

He gave her a sideways glance. "You think you're going to get rid of me now, don't you?"

Unsure of what to say, Ariel began straightening up the mat samples on the table. It was almost as if he had read her mind, she thought ruefully. Well, he could flirt all he wanted. She wasn't about to go the way of other divorcées she'd seen who took to flirting with younger men out of desperation.

He was studying one painting from a distance, then moved in to examine it in detail. "It says 'Ryan' in the corner," he said at last, "but it's sure not Red's work and it's also not in the Rose Saunders mode."

"I painted that," she told him. It was of a graveyard, the church beyond barely discernible in the fog. She had painted it years ago when she was still married and painting for her own pleasure.

"You can paint something like this and you're painting *daisies*?"

The note of incredulity in his voice angered her. "People aren't exactly standing in line to buy paintings of graveyards," she shot back.

"People weren't standing in line to buy *Toledo*, either, but you didn't see El Greco switch to painting flowers in designer colors."

She was a little nonplussed at how serious he sounded. "I'm hardly El Greco," she said sarcastically.

"None of us is, but that doesn't mean we don't aspire to it."

"Look, I'm giving the customers what they want," she protested.

"Which is the same excuse for peddling all the inferior merchandise around. If all the people ever see is Rose Saunders's brand of commercial claptrap, how are they supposed to know any better?''

She said, "Look, I told you I have two daughters to support."

"Then why don't you put them up for adoption and get down to some real work? You could be a real artist if you gave yourself half a chance."

His suggestion was so outrageous she had to laugh. "The hell with children, true art's the only thing that matters in this world, is that it?"

He smiled. "I guess I got carried away. You seem to have a marked facility for putting me on my soapbox. It's your attitude that's the problem, not your kids, anyway."

"No need to apologize. I like a good argument."

"I'm not apologizing—I'll defend my views to the death. I have a better idea, though. Why don't you close up the shop for a while and take a break. I'll buy you a beer at Clancy's."

"I couldn't do that—"

"Sure you can, you're the owner, aren't you? Come on, take the phone off the hook, get out of that ugly smock you're wearing, and let's go celebrate your new line of custom framing. We can sit outside and you'll get some sun."

Scott was moving around the table toward her, making her aware of the fact that they were alone in the shop without much possibility of interruption. She could smell him again, that male scent of his combined with sun and salt water and suntan oil. She thought dazedly he ought to put more clothes on in public and not go around half-naked, but then he smiled at her and the smile didn't reach his eyes, which remained quite serious. He reached out, causing her to back into the wall. He placed his hands on her shoulders, his touch flooding her with a sudden, inexplicable warmth, as though the sun he had absorbed was now flowing into her.

This is ridiculous, thought Ariel. *I should say something, maybe make a joke, somehow break the tension between us. He probably thinks it's sexual tension, but it's not—it's just that I'm not at ease with men anymore.* She looked up at him, trying unsuccessfully to read what was in his eyes, then looked back down in confusion. Her eyes were on a level with his chest, which was matted with curly hair that formed a vee as it disappeared into the waistband of his jeans.

She looked up at him. "Look, Scott, I'm thirty-eight years old." Unfortunately, he didn't spring away in horror at her news.

"If that was meant to discourage me, it failed."

She sighed and tried to assume her motherly air. "What are you, about thirty?"

Her motherly air seemed to be having about as much effect on him as it had on her daughters. He was smiling. "You're continuing to place importance on all the wrong things, Ariel."

Well, he's been warned, she thought, as she felt his hands go to the top button of her smock, feeling the warmth of his palms against the pulse in her neck. She could feel her heart pounding as he slowly began to undo the buttons on her smock, his hands brushing lightly against her breasts as he did so. Flustered, she looked at his lips, not smiling now but hard and firm, and she suddenly wondered what they would feel like

pressed against her own. She felt the almost impercep-
tible tilt of her body toward his—and then the moment
was shattered. The buttons were undone and nothing
untoward had happened; he was merely helping her off
with her smock. She should have felt relief, but she
didn't.

Frustrated old lady, she derided herself. *The first pre-
sentable man to make a move on you and you go to pieces.
And as it turned out, he wasn't even making a move, anyway.*

She stood there feeling foolish as his eyes surveyed
her in her faded purple overalls and pink T-shirt. She
could feel her face flush and the hair on her forehead
suddenly become damp. She wanted to brush it back,
but she was afraid it would be construed as a nervous
gesture. Not that that wouldn't be an accurate appraisal.

"I'm surprised Red didn't paint you," he said at last.
"If I had you around, I sure would."

She swallowed. "Dad didn't go in for portrait painting," she answered nervously.

"It wasn't portrait painting I had in mind," he said,
his eyes admiring.

"He's my father," she said, shocked by his un-
spoken suggestion.

"Yes, but I'm not." He obviously enjoyed unnerving
her. Damn, even her daughter would be able to handle
the situation better than she was doing. But then, her
daughter had probably been getting a lot more practice
at this.

Ariel thought quickly. "I think I'll take you up on
that offer of a beer," she said, aware of the electricity
between them. If they left the shop, some of that electricity was bound to dissipate.

She went to the back of the shop to take the phone off the hook and grab her straw bag. By the time she returned he had penned a sign and was taping it to her front door. BE BACK LATER—MAYBE, the sign read, making her chuckle.

"No 'maybe' about it," she said firmly.

"We'll see about that," she heard him muttering under his breath as she locked the door to the store, but she decided to ignore the challenge. She would have one beer with him, that was all, and then she'd go back to the shop and try to do something about rearranging the storefront to make it more inviting to potential customers. She was a businesswoman, not a dilettante, and she wasn't going to make a habit out of closing up her shop on a whim to have drinks with customers.

She glanced up at him as he walked by her side. Good grief, why was such a good-looking young man even interested in having a beer with her? People would probably think she was his mother walking with him. That thought did nothing to cheer her up.

At Clancy's, which was situated across the street from the beach, Scott found them a table out of doors and ordered them each a Coors without asking her, something her husband had invariably done and which had never failed to annoy her. One of the joys of being single was being able to order for herself. She decided, however, it wasn't worth making an issue over, particularly since she'd never be having a drink with him again. And anyway, she liked Coors.

Ariel's eyes went to the ocean, and she watched the waves break against the shore. When she and her daughters had moved to Seal Beach to take over her father's business, she had thought she would have the beach to herself early in the morning and had looked forward to solitary walks before the girls got up. She was soon disabused of that notion when she found that surfers converged on Seal Beach from miles around, the early morning hours being allotted to them before the beach became crowded with swimmers and sunbathers. Even on the coldest and rainiest of mornings, surfers, wearing wet suits to protect themselves from the elements, laid siege on the beach. Nonetheless, she found she enjoyed visiting the beach in the early morning hours, watching the surfers as they rode the waves.

Her eyes went to Scott. To her he looked more like a surfer than an artist with his firmly muscled body, deep tan and sun-bleached hair. It was her experience that as a rule artists were an unhealthy-looking lot, seldom emerging from their studios until the sun set, and then only to sit around sidewalk cafés and drink.

"I should be flattered by all the attention, but somehow I think your thoughts are elsewhere," Scott said, jarring her out of her reverie and then, when she realized she had been staring, averting her eyes from his body.

"I was just thinking you look more like a surfer than an artist," she confessed.

He laughed. "I haven't surfed since high school days. If you're referring to the tan, I take time out from working to run on the beach. An artist needs some exercise after spending long hours at the easel."

Ariel agreed, but no one would ever have been able to convince her father of that. Red Ryan's idea of exercise was bending his elbow at the neighborhood bar and endlessly discussing art with his cronies, of which Scott was apparently one, she remembered.

"Do you surf?" he was asking her.

"No. We didn't live near the ocean when I was growing up, and my parents didn't consider visits to beaches to be a necessity."

"You could always learn now," he suggested.

"At my age?" she asked, scandalized.

"You're not quite ready for a rocking chair yet, you know. People your age do occasionally participate in physical activities."

She was saved from responding to that remark by the arrival of their beer.

Scott raised his glass to her in a toast. "Here's to your new line of custom framing. May it be a resounding success, monetarily, of course."

She was lifting her glass in answer when three young women walked by, all with long, blond hair parted in the middle, all wearing the skimpiest of bikinis, and all superficially resembling her oldest daughter. Seeing Scott they stopped, one of them asking him where he'd been keeping himself, the others dismissing Ariel with brief glances.

As the girls vied for his attention, Ariel watched him rise to the occasion. Bestowing his considerable charm on all three, his banter was casual, his laughter infectious. She could certainly see why the girls were attracted to him, if she were ten years younger she'd probably be interested herself.

The girls departed, but then other people continually stopped as they passed to say hello to Scott, the men giving Ariel expectant glances as though waiting for an introduction, one that never came. She figured she must have taken on an aura of attractiveness just by being in his company.

Finally Scott shrugged and threw some money on the table. "Come on—I'll walk you back. There's no way we're going to get any talking done here."

"You must know everyone in Seal Beach," Ariel remarked as she got to her feet.

"Just about, but then, it's a small town and I've lived here all my life."

She had to quicken her pace to keep up with his long strides. "I'd like to thank you again, Scott—you've been very helpful."

"You can thank me tonight over dinner."

"No, I'm sorry.... I can't." Her response was automatic.

"Don't tell me you're going to keep the gallery open? You've got to eat, you know."

When she didn't reply he said, "How about tomorrow night?"

Her first impulse was to say yes, which surprised her. Then reason took over. "Thanks, Scott, but no."

"You living with somebody?" he asked her.

"No."

"Going with someone?"

She shook her head.

"Then what's the problem?"

"I'm just not interested."

He abruptly stopped walking and turned to her, taking hold of her chin with one hand and tipping her face up to look her in the eyes. "In me or going out in general?"

She gave him a level look. "In either."

"I don't believe that for a minute. There was something between us the moment we met; you felt it as much as I did."

"I'm afraid it was just nervousness on my part."

Scott frowned, but he seemed to accept her explanation. They continued to walk in silence until they reached the door to her shop. She was reaching inside her bag for her keys when he put his hands on her shoulders and looked down at her.

"There's no reason why we can't be friends, is there?"

Ariel smiled, happy that she hadn't antagonized him, after all. "No. No reason at all." It would be nice to have Scott for a friend, someone who could give her advice on her business, stop by the shop sometimes to say hello. It probably wouldn't even hurt to have lunch with him occasionally, or even a beer.

"Good!" With that, he leaned down and covered her mouth with his, catching her completely off guard. She was too startled to move as his rough, demanding lips urged a response from her, a response she felt quite naturally coming to life inside her until maturity and good sense surfaced, and she quickly pushed him away.

"I thought you said we could be friends," she said, feeling slightly betrayed.

His eyes were gleaming. "You didn't really think I'd give up that easily, did you?" He was on his bike, moving it over the curb and into traffic before she could react, blowing her a kiss over his shoulder as he rode swiftly down Main Street.

"Mother!" came a shocked voice from behind her. "You kissed that man!"

Chapter Two

Startled, she dropped the keys to the shop and had to bend to pick them up. She felt unaccountably guilty, which was nonsense; she hadn't done anything wrong.

"I didn't kiss him, Nicole—he kissed me," Ariel defended herself to her daughter, "and I certainly didn't ask for it."

"What were you doing with him, anyway?"

"He's a customer."

"Why's the shop closed?" Nicole asked suspiciously.

She unlocked the door and marched inside. "Because I got an urge to close the place and spend the afternoon kissing strange men, all right?"

Nicole followed her inside, trailing sand in her wake. "He looked awfully young to me. Who is he?" Her voice wasn't exactly a whine, but it was bordering on it.

"He looked awfully young to me, too. Where's your sister?"

"Don't change the subject, Mother."

"I thought we'd exhausted it," Ariel retorted a trifle sharply. "Where's Jody?"

"Where else? Playing urban guerrilla with her retarded friends," Nicole said disapprovingly.

Perhaps that was preferable to playing nymphet of the beach, thought Ariel, eyeing her daughter's brief bikini. Nicole seemed to be getting lovelier by the minute, looking more mature than her almost-sixteen years.

"Will you watch the shop for me for a few minutes while I run over to Sutton's?"

"Who is he, Mother?" Nicole persisted.

"His name's Scott Campbell."

"He was certainly good-looking."

"Yes. He's a very nice-looking young man."

"Why is he interested in *you*?"

"Look, will you watch the shop for me? I won't be long."

Nicole gave a martyred sigh. "Go ahead, run over and tell Sutton all about it. I never get to hear anything."

"Nicole, there's nothing to hear."

"I'll bet," she heard Nicole mutter as she disappeared into the bathroom. Ariel knew that Nicole would spend the next half hour combing her long hair. Nicole had reached the age where her looks were her primary concern, which was ridiculous, since the girl had nothing to be concerned about.

In the time she'd been running the gallery, Sutton's boutique had become her refuge and the woman herself her best friend. Divorced like her, with a daughter in college, the older woman had helped Ariel out in more ways than she could ever repay. Whatever problem seemed to come up, Sutton always seemed to have been through the same thing before and would have accurate and useful advice to offer. And, happily, she delighted in dispensing advice.

Her boutique featured one-of-a-kind sundresses and

bikinis that had been designed by Sutton and that were clearly out of Ariel's price range, but she loved looking at them anyway. Sutton, with her slim model's build, was her own best advertisement for her dresses, never failing to sell anything she wore around the shop, sometimes selling it right off her back.

She was in the back room sewing when Ariel entered and paused in the showroom, looking at some new items displayed before she joined her friend.

"I saw you," were Sutton's first words.

"You saw me what?"

"I saw you with that gorgeous man."

Ariel sat down in a wicker chair and took the proffered cup of coffee. "So did Nicole. So did the whole town, probably."

"How come I haven't heard of him?"

"Because I just met him. Anyway, there's nothing to hear."

Sutton gave her a measured look. "It didn't look to me as though there's nothing to hear. I mean, if that much was going on outside your shop, God only knows what was going on inside."

"Nothing happened inside, believe me."

"What a shame."

"How old did he look to you, Sutton? Did you get a good look?"

Sutton chuckled. "As good as possible without running across the street. I'd say he looked as if he were in his prime."

"Considering the source, that would mean about eighteen."

"No, he looked older than that. But don't knock the young, Ariel, you know not of what you speak."

"If I wanted a son I'd adopt one," Ariel answered, tongue in cheek.

"Who's talking about a son?"

"Doesn't it bother you going out with younger guys?" She'd asked the question before and gotten the answer before, but somehow today she needed to hear it again.

"If it doesn't bother them, why should it bother me? Anyway, although I may look like forty-three, I sure as hell don't feel like it."

"I feel thirty-eight."

"But you don't look it."

"I look it," Ariel affirmed dryly.

"I'm not going to get into that argument with you again," said Sutton, lighting one of her pastel-colored cigarettes. "Anyway, what happened? Are you going out with him?"

Ariel shook her head.

"Did he ask you?"

"He asked me. And he's not very good at taking no for an answer."

"With his looks, he's probably never run into rejection before."

"But why me?"

"Why not? Plenty of men would take you out if you gave them a chance."

"You're the one who's always telling me there aren't any good men around."

"Ah, but you notice I didn't say 'good' men. I just said 'men.'"

"I don't get it. All the men our age are running around with the twenty-year-olds. Why would a younger guy pick me?"

"Maybe he liked your mind."

"All we did was argue."

"Arguing can be very erotic."

Ariel looked at her friend to see if Sutton was serious. She was. "You might have a point. I enjoy a good argument."

"Sure you do, that's healthy. You'd probably enjoy a good hop in the sack, too. Unless you're really serious about spending the rest of your life living like a nun. Sans habit, of course."

"You think I should go out with him?"

"I think you should stop analyzing everything and just go with your feelings for a change. Do you want to go out with him?"

"I don't know."

"Did you want to go out with him when he was kissing you?"

"Yes."

"That was a very reluctant 'yes.'"

"I don't know, Sutton. He's awfully sexy."

"Gee, that's a real disadvantage, isn't it? Would you want to go out with a guy who wasn't sexy?"

"I didn't find my husband particularly sexy."

"And you didn't have a particularly good marriage, either, did you?"

"I don't know, Sutton," Ariel said, troubled. "Nicole dates. That's the age when you're supposed to date. I'm too old for this nonsense."

"Then circumvent dating—just have an affair."

"It's the sex I feel like circumventing."

"Hell's bells, Ariel, you're acting like a frightened virgin."

"That's the problem. I can't act like a frightened virgin. I could always pull that when I was young, but now I have nothing to fall back on. Once you've been married, you're fair game. Any guy's going to expect to go to bed with me."

"You can always say no."

"I'm not so sure of that," Ariel said.

"Nobody's going to force you. If they can't get satisfaction from you, they'll go elsewhere."

"I'm not worried about being forced. I'm worried about saying yes just to be polite."

"You're kidding?"

"No, I'm not. I can just see me getting into the kind of situation where I'd say yes, go along with it, just to avoid a scene. I don't remember how to handle myself on a date, Sutton."

"It would probably come back to you."

"If it did, it probably wouldn't work anymore. The dating game has changed radically, or so I hear."

"That it has," Sutton agreed, "but in a lot of ways it's changed for the better. You don't have to play at being something you're not anymore. It's a lot more honest, I think."

"I guess I'm just scared."

"I know you are. But it's like getting back in a car and driving after you've had an accident. What's the worst that can happen, another accident?"

"You could always get killed."

"Don't be so literal," Sutton snapped. "In a car maybe, but not from sex."

"I'm just not ready for this."

Sutton gave an audible sigh. "Then why did you come running over here to tell me about this man?"

"I wanted your advice."

"And you got it. What you do with it now is your problem."

Ariel got up and shoved her hands in the pockets of her overalls. "Thanks, Sutton."

"What are you going to do?"

"Think about it."

"What're you doing tonight?"

"I have my class with Rose."

"Want to meet for a drink after?"

Ariel shook her head. "Nicole's going out, and I don't want to leave Jody home alone that late."

"God, no—she might terrorize the town."

Ariel chuckled. "I'm beginning to think we're living under siege."

"Let me know when you come to a decision."

"You'll probably be the first to know," Ariel assured her.

No customers had come in, the telephone hadn't rung, and Nicole was still in the bathroom playing with her hair when Ariel returned to the shop.

"So, did Sutton hear all of the juicy stuff?"

"Nicole, why don't you find your sister and pick up a pizza? I'm going to close up soon."

The mention of pizza still worked its magic, sparing Ariel from having to answer any more questions. And that was another good reason for her not dating—Nicole. She wasn't quite sure what the girl's reaction would be, but she wasn't sure she wanted to find out.

When Ariel was first divorced, Nicole seemed to be waiting for her to start dating, the way divorced mothers of her friends were doing. When Ariel instead showed no interest in men, Nicole seemed to visibly relax, and now Ariel was afraid the child had her on

some kind of pedestal. She had overheard Nicole brag-
ging to her friends that *her* mother wouldn't go out
with men, that *her* mother still had some dignity. Ariel
had never thought of herself as being dignified, but
after hearing that said with a tone of pride in Nicole's
voice, she realized she'd been trying to live up to that
image. And that image would surely shatter if she were
to begin dating a younger man. Anyway, weren't there
only two reasons to date younger men? Desperation
and—as Sutton put it—great sex? Well, she didn't feel
desperate, and so far she wasn't climbing the walls over
the lack of sex. Her life was fine the way it was. And
she had enough problems just trying to support herself
and her two daughters without looking for added com-
plications. And if the custom framing portion of the
business began to pick up, they could start eating steaks
once in a while instead of pizza and hamburgers. Steak,
at the moment, sounded a lot better to her than sex.

Despite her father's opinion—and she deeply admired
his talent—Ariel thought Rose Saunders was a wonderful painter. Her work might be slick and commercial,
and the pictures might be done in decorator colors, but
they were pure pleasure to look at, and a lot of people
were very proud to have them hanging in their homes.
Maybe she was a "lady" painter and concentrated primarily on florals, but Ariel thought that a vase of
flowers was every bit as artistic as a bottle of wine and a
bunch of onions, which many of the male artists
seemed to set such store by.

She also liked Rose as a person. She was one of a
kind, probably considered an eccentric by her neighbors up on the hill where she lived. Seal Beach was

divided into two parts: The first was "old town," which was between Pacific Coast Highway and the ocean, and it consisted of Main Street with its three blocks of small stores and restaurants, and the streets branched away from it lined with small old houses and an occasional apartment building; the other part of the town was referred to as "the hill" and was the several blocks running north of the highway. The hill was where the more affluent people lived, with the exception of the lucky few who actually owned beachfront property.

Rose lived in an enormous round house on the top of the hill. When Ariel first saw it from the outside, she had wondered why an artist would choose to live in a round house, when it would be impossible to hang pictures on the walls. Once inside, however, she saw that the walls were straight and didn't correspond to the shape of the house. The house's detached three-car garage had been converted into a studio for Rose, and it was here that she held her painting classes.

Ariel admired Rose as a person as well as an artist. Although she was in her fifties, she had the tall, slim body of a girl and wore her graying blond hair in a long braid down her back. Ariel had heard she had children who were married as well as a couple of teenagers who were still at home, and the house always seemed to be filled with young people and grandchildren along with dogs and cats and even a couple of rabbits lived in the yard. When Rose held her class, a sign reading DO NOT DISTURB—EVER was hung on the garage door, and the housekeeper had strict instructions that she was to handle any emergencies without the benefit of Rose's advice.

This evening, as the class had been promised, they

were to begin a painting of the San Juan Capistrano mission. Ariel knew what her father would have to say about her painting the mission, but she also knew that these mission paintings proliferated in the weekend art shows at the shopping malls. And she also knew that they were extremely good sellers, and that was the name of the game. If the sale of a mission painting paid for the groceries for a month, there was no way she was going to knock it.

Rose was already sketching in the drawing on an extra large canvas by the time Ariel arrived at class. She took a seat in front of one of the empty easels, exchanged hellos with her neighbors, and then began to lay out the colors Rose had listed on the blackboard. Sometimes, if the picture they were to paint was a simple one, Rose would demonstrate first, finishing her own painting as they watched before they began on their own. A mission, however, took a pretty detailed drawing to begin with, and for this painting she told them they would do it together.

Rose quickly finished her sketch and turned around to face the class. She gave them a little talk on perspective, demonstrating on the blackboard. This was the first time the class had done a painting where perspective was needed. Ariel, who had learned about perspective years ago, began on her drawing and soon found that the graduated arches weren't as easy to execute as she had thought. However, Rose was telling the class that mistakes in perspective on the arches could be disguised by means of bougainvillea hanging off the edges.

Rose walked around the classroom after she had finished her talk, checking on the drawings. When she got to Ariel's, she pointed out only one small change to be made and then told her she could start on the sky.

"Don't put in one of your busy ones, though," Rose warned. "Just a clear blue so you don't detract from the mission."

Ariel nodded and began filling in the empty space with a slightly muted ultramarine, fading it out as it reached the horizon. She then sat back and waited for the class to catch up to her. She was anxious to get started on the building itself. She knew Rose used a palette knife to achieve the effect of stucco, and she was looking forward to learning knife technique. They got no farther that night, however, than laying in the underpainting, which had to dry before they went on to the next step.

When the class ended, Ariel asked permission to leave her unfinished canvas in Rose's garage. It was the largest she had ever painted—twenty-four by forty-eight—and she didn't think she'd be able to get it into the back seat of her Volkswagen.

When she got home Nicole was still out, as expected, and Jody was already asleep, which was unexpected. Ariel's younger daughter had taken to sleeping in a pup tent on the floor of the bedroom, and Ariel checked in on her before she went downstairs to the shop to see if she could recreate the sketch of the mission on her own. She didn't have a canvas that large, so she sketched in the work she had done in class on a twelve by twenty-four canvas and repeated the underpainting they had done in class. Tomorrow, when it dried, she would experiment and see whether she could do a mission on her own without Rose's instructions.

Around midnight she heard a car pull up in the alley

behind the shop and assumed it was Nicole's date bringing her home. She gave them a few minutes and then, when she heard the car door close, she let herself out the back of the shop and met her daughter as she was climbing the stairs to their apartment.

"Did you have a good time?" she asked.

"Ummm." Nicole was generally noncommittal rather than forthcoming about her dates. Since Ariel had been the same way at her age, she didn't think much about it.

"How about you?" Nicole asked her mother. "Did you see Mr. Wonderful again?"

Ariel ignored the question. Two could play at the game of being noncommittal. Anyway, she hadn't seen Scott again, and she was rather sorry Nicole had reminded her of him. Now she knew she'd start thinking of him, and she found that thinking about men was as nonproductive as thinking could possibly get.

Nicole was peeling an orange in the kitchen when Ariel went in to put on some water for tea. She eyed her daughter's mouth and almost smiled. When she was in high school and on a date with a boy, she would apply a fresh coat of lipstick before going into the house, which was probably a dead giveaway to her parents. These days the girls didn't wear lipstick to begin with, which made the deception so much easier.

"We saw a good movie, Mom, you should see it."

"What was it about?"

"This divorced woman with three kids. It was pretty interesting."

"I'm a divorced woman with two kids. I don't need to see a movie."

"It was how she solved all her problems."

Ariel thought she could probably have written the movie script herself. "How did she solve them?"

"She married this rich guy in the end."

Ariel burst out laughing. It was no secret that Nicole preferred being affluent to being relatively poor. The worst shock to her older daughter had been moving from a two-story house to a small apartment above a store. For the first few months they lived there, she had been embarrassed to bring her school friends home.

"It wasn't funny, Mother—it was very realistically done."

"How did she manage to meet this rich man?"

"She met him on a vacation in Acapulco."

"Well, if I could afford a vacation in Acapulco—"

"*She* could afford it because *she* got lots of alimony." Nicole gave her a superior look.

"You know how I feel about alimony, Nicole."

"I just don't think it's fair to us."

"Honey, if your father paid me any more than he does, he wouldn't have enough left to live on."

"He could always get his old job back."

"But that was the whole point of the divorce. He wanted to try a new life-style."

"Well, what about us? Maybe we liked our old life-style!" Nicole flounced out of the kitchen before Ariel could reply. Not that there was anything new to say. The only thing in her favor was that the girls had learned to love living at the beach. They might miss their old house in Anaheim, but they certainly didn't miss the area. Ariel didn't even miss the house, but then, she had been the one who had had to clean it. She didn't think she'd ever want to live in a big house again.

She would have liked to take her tea out onto the balcony that overlooked Main Street, but the door to the balcony was off the girls' bedroom and she didn't want to disturb them. Instead, she went into the living room and opened the sofa bed. She'd read for a while as her mind relaxed from the day's pressures.

She took off her sneakers and jeans and got into bed in just her T-shirt and bikini panties. Joan Didion's latest book didn't hold her attention. She finally put it aside and turned out the light, thinking with amusement of her conversation with her daughter. Nicole would obviously like her to remarry again and definitely to a rich man. On the other hand, her daughter didn't seem to want her to date. Conversely, Sutton would be delighted to see her start to date but would certainly view remarriage as a disaster. Both of them were in agreement that being single rather than married had far more advantages than disadvantages.

If her reaction to Scott was any indication, perhaps it was time for her to start seeing men. Her body obviously hadn't forgotten what her mind had managed to sublimate. She had always enjoyed sex during her marriage; indeed, it was the only part she missed. If she had been divorced in her twenties rather than her thirties, she probably would have begun dating fairly soon after her divorce. But thirty-eight sounded so—old. She couldn't even imagine a man being interested in someone her age unless he was considerably older himself. And men considerably older than herself didn't even look remotely interesting to her.

It was all academic, anyway. Men weren't calling her for dates, she was seldom anywhere where she met available men, and Scott had probably been a fluke. He no doubt had plenty of young women friends and only saw her as a momentary diversion, perhaps a challenge when she didn't fall all over him.

But if he asked her out again, she might accept. Just to see what it was like, dating again. And when he saw her situation, met her two daughters, he'd assuredly back off anyway. At least it would give her something to talk about with Sutton; discussions about men were now so one-sided it made her feel like an old bore.

Furthermore, she had spent enough time thinking about men. What would happen would happen, but right now she needed her sleep. She closed her eyes and willed her mind to rest.

Ariel half expected to see Scott pull up in front of her shop on his bike on Thursday. After all, he had said he didn't give up easily. But the entire day passed with no sign of him.

Not that she wasn't constantly reminded of him. She had an almost steady stream of customers in the shop that day, all of them as a result of the sign he had printed and placed in the window. Several of the customers told Ariel how pleased they were not to have to go into Long Beach for their custom framing. A couple of them were friends of her father, and they mentioned what a good idea it was to give artists a discount, then stayed to chat for a while about Red's precipitous marriage.

By the time she closed the shop that evening she had done more business in one day than she had done in the previous two months combined. She was almost sorry Scott hadn't stopped by so that she could thank him.

In between customers she had worked on her painting of the mission, but it didn't go as well as she had hoped. The red tile roof lacked dimension and she couldn't seem to get the hang of painting stucco. She finally set it aside to work on after her next class with Rose.

That night Nicole was invited to a beach party and planned to eat there, so Ariel took Jody to the Wooden Shoe for hamburgers. Afterward, her daughter wheedled her into seeing the surfing movie at the Bay Theater. Ariel realized that she was an anomaly as they stood in line to get tickets; like most of the theatergoers she was dressed in jeans and a T-shirt, but the rest were obviously surfers and not one of them appeared to be older than thirty. Jody, in her battle fatigues and canteen hanging from her belt, fit in better than she did.

Despite her earlier misgivings, Ariel enjoyed the movie thoroughly. It was beautifully filmed, the scenery was gorgeous, and if she found herself looking too long and hard at some of the young men's bodies, she reasoned she wasn't the only one doing so. And it was a lot more entertaining than watching a movie about a divorcée.

Afterward they walked down to Mother's for ice cream cones. As they were walking along the beach eating them, Jody said, out of the blue, "Nicole says she saw you kissing a man, but I didn't believe her. She was making it up, wasn't she?"

Explaining to a teenager who was nightly kissing her own boyfriend was one thing. But how did one explain to an eleven-year-old?

"He was just teasing me, honey—it didn't mean anything."

"Oh, yeah. Some of the boys in our class try to do that. Two of them held Lisa down while another one kissed her on the mouth. It was really gross—I almost barfed when it happened."

Well, that wasn't quite the image she wanted Jody to have of kissing, even though it let her off the hook effectively. "Kissing can be very nice, Jody, when you like somebody."

"I'm never going to do it!"

"I think you'll change your mind when you get older."

"I'm never going to change my mind. You know what Nicole told me? She says that sometimes boys kiss with their mouths open! Isn't that disgusting?"

She found she could relate far better to Jody than to Nicole, having been a tomboy herself as a girl. "Actually, it sounds more disgusting than it is," she said.

"Did you kiss Daddy like that?"

"Of course I did."

Jody gave her a disbelieving look. "Did you ever kiss anyone else like that?"

"Honey, it's not as bad as it sounds. When two people have strong feelings for each other, they do lots of things that might sound strange to you now."

"If you're talking about sex, I know all about it. And I don't like the sound of any of it."

Ariel couldn't help laughing, even when she saw Jody's answering scowl. "How do you know all about sex?"

"We had a movie at school. I almost barfed!"

Ariel hoped it was better than the movie she had

been shown at the same age. That one had left her with more questions than answers, and she could remember that for days afterward she'd hardly been able to look her parents in the eye.

"Well, just remember this conversation in a few years' time, and see if you still feel the same."

"I'm always going to feel the same," Jody said adamantly.

"But you like boys, don't you? I notice all your friends are boys."

"Yeah, but they're friends. They wouldn't dare mess around with me or I'd total them."

Ariel dropped the subject. One daughter at a time interested in the opposite sex was quite enough. For that matter, one in the family interested in the opposite sex was quite enough. She was sure her newly awakened interest in men would soon die down.

Chapter Three

Windflower delivered Ariel's custom framing at five o'clock on Friday. At five-twenty Scott appeared in her shop with a large frame under his arm and a big grin on his face. Ariel almost didn't recognize him at first, as he was fully clothed. Not only was he fully clothed but he looked almost distinguished in fawn-colored slacks, a white shirt open at the neck, and a navy blue sport jacket. He was even wearing shoes. The clothes made him look a little older. Not that it mattered. Old or young, she just wasn't interested. Nonetheless, Ariel felt grubby in comparison in her paint-stained jeans and shirt.

"Hi, beautiful, did you miss me?"

As it had only been two days since she had seen him, she didn't think his remark worthy of a reply.

She glanced down at the frame he was holding. "Did you bring in a painting?"

"Nope."

She shrugged and turned away. If he was trying to be mysterious, she wasn't going to let him arouse her curiosity.

"It's a surprise—I'll show you later."

"If you'll just watch as I fit one of your graphics, you won't have to be here later," she told him.

"Don't worry, I couldn't hang around and bother you tonight even if I wanted to. It's a big night tonight—the Laguna Beach Art Festival is opening."

And that he had a big date for it she was sure, judging by the way he was dressed. No doubt with one of those lovely young blondes who hung around him.

"Your frames are in the back," she said, moving through the arched doorway that led to the rear of the shop. She removed a frame from its brown wrapping-paper protection and then found the corresponding graphic. When she was ready to begin fitting, she noticed that Scott was standing by her shoulder.

She took a piece of glass from a carton, positioned it against the inside of the frame, and then made a mark where to cut it.

"You can cut it like that in the frame," he remarked.

"No, I can't. I always break it that way," she said shortly, wondering why she felt compelled to be rude to him.

"Do you want me—"

"No, I don't!" She cut the glass in what she thought was a quick and expert manner, and then reached over and found the mat board she had previously cut so that the fitting wouldn't take her all night. Turning the mat board over, she positioned the graphic and was reaching for the masking tape when Scott grabbed her hand.

"That's a no-no," he said, laughing when she wrenched her hand from his grip. "I knew you were going to need instructions."

"That's the way they taught me at Windflower," she muttered.

"Yes, but those were no doubt prints—these are original graphics. You don't tape down graphics or they lose some of their value."

"And these are priceless, I suppose," she snapped, regarding him stonily.

"My, my. We're in a temper tonight, aren't we?"

Ariel knew that he was behaving perfectly politely while she was acting like a temperamental artist. And could it possibly have had anything to do with the fact that he was going out tonight and not with her? If so, she was certainly acting childishly and he didn't deserve it.

"I'm sorry," she apologized. "It's just that it makes me nervous having someone watch me while I'm fitting." That was an outright lie, but it was better than no apology at all.

"Anyway, to answer your question, no, these aren't priceless. Someday maybe, but not now. You should, however, learn to frame them correctly." He reached into his jacket pocket and brought out an envelope filled with glassine papers. "Here, use these," he said. "Just moisten them and stick them on."

He watched silently as she washed the glass, put the matted graphic inside, shot the diamond points into the frame to hold the picture and glass in, and then glued brown paper to the back.

"Do you want it wired?" she asked him.

"Of course."

She screwed in the eyelets and then strung the wire across. When she was finished, she presented it to him. "Is it okay?"

He looked it over carefully. "I couldn't have done it better myself. Faster, but not better."

"There's something I want to tell you," Ariel said to him, knowing that she owed him that.

"You've changed your mind and want to go out with me?"

"No," she said, ignoring his hopeful expression.

"You have a yen for my body, and we can't keep meeting like this?"

Her good intentions were dissolving fast. "I just wanted to tell you my custom framing business has been doing great ever since you put that sign in the window."

"Business. And here I thought you were going to get personal," Scott said, but there was laughter in his eyes.

She had to smile at his single-mindedness. Still, now that she saw him again she couldn't really believe he was actually interested in her. He was far too desirable to want to go out with a middle-aged woman. It had been a nice fantasy while it lasted, but she just couldn't take it seriously once she was in his presence again.

"Ah, I see by your smile that you're softening toward me."

Her smile slowly dissolved. "Scott, couldn't we just be friends?"

"No way, Ariel. What I feel when I'm near you is not what I feel when I'm with my friends. But we certainly could be friendly." He reached out for her, but she moved around the fitting table, out of his reach.

"Then the answer to that is not to get near me," she pointed out to him.

Something shifted in the blue-green depths of his eyes. "Oh, no—I don't think that's the answer. And I don't think you think so, either." He moved around the table, but she kept moving too, until it occurred to her that they looked like two children playing keep-away—and at the thought of that she burst out laughing.

He stopped, then also started to laugh. "You're right, we're behaving like kids. Nor is this the time and the place. But when I do make my move—"

She waited for him to complete his sentence, but he just stood there shaking his head, the overhead lights making his hair gleam like gold.

"What's the surprise you had for later?" she finally asked, once again feeling the need to dissipate the tension that existed between them.

He moved toward the front of the shop. "Come on out and I'll show you."

When she caught up with him he was holding the large, framed sign in front of him, a big smile on his face.

ONE-DAY WORKSHOPS
WITH SCOTT CAMPBELL
SATURDAYS 10–5
$175
INQUIRE WITHIN

She read it over twice before she looked up at him. He looked so pleased with himself, like Jody when she'd done something terrific, that she had to smile. "I don't understand."

"What's to understand? I've decided I'll teach some workshops here. How many easels do you have in the back?"

"Twelve."

"Good. One for me, one for you, and that leaves ten students you can sign up for each workshop. I thought I'd give six of them."

"Scott, nobody is going to pay $175 for one lesson, even if it is all day. Rose only charges $5 for three hours."

"You'd be surprised how crazy some people are."

"I don't know," she said, shaking her head.

"You can't say no, I've already put an ad in the paper, the price of which you can reimburse me for out of the profits."

"What profits?" Ariel asked, aghast.

"The way I figure it, I'll take $100 from each student and you get $75. That—plus the painting supplies and frames you'll sell to them—you should make a tidy little sum."

Ariel did some quick figuring in her head and visions of economic freedom began to overwhelm her. Then practicality took over. It was unlikely there were ten crazy people out there willing to pay $175 for one lesson, even if Picaso came back from the grave to teach it.

Scott was already arranging the sign in the window alongside the custom framing one. He had obviously gone to a lot of trouble and she didn't want to sound discouraging, so she decided to wait. When no one signed up, that would tell him better than she could that it just wasn't feasible. But if it did work, heaven knows she could use the money, just as he probably could. And spending Saturdays with him wouldn't be all that hard to take, either.

Scott walked back to her. "They're definitely going to have to buy supplies from you because I work on square canvases, which none of them are going to have, and I use a large palette knife, which very few of them will have. And not all of them will have the colors I require." He grabbed a pad and pencil from the counter and began making out a list. "I only use five colors, so get in a couple of boxes of each. And a couple of dozen knives to start. And have them make up thirty canvases thirty-six by thirty-six."

"And where am I supposed to get all of this?" She didn't particularly like the way he was taking charge. Shouldn't he be deferring more to her since she was older? And therefore wiser?

"Call Grumbacher in Long Beach," Scott advised her. "They'll have it out to you by Tuesday. They'll extend credit, too—you won't have to pay for the supplies until the end of the month."

Ariel tried to say it as gently as possible. "And what if no one signs up and I'm stuck with all that stuff?"

He gave her a look of astonishment. "You don't have any faith in me, Ariel. Didn't I get you custom framing customers?"

"Yes, but that was different."

"I'll make you a guarantee. If I don't fill the workshops, I'll buy the supplies from you myself. At cost, of course. Deal?"

"You don't need all of that," Ariel protested.

"Maybe not the knives, but the rest of it I can use. Oh, and order a couple of cartons of linseed oil."

Ariel added it to the list, then shook her head, bemused. "Why are you taking such an interest in my business?"

His eyes first took in the thin blue T-shirt that molded itself to her curves, then went down to her narrow waist and curved derriere in the slim-cut jeans she wore. "Oh, it's not your business I'm interested in, Ariel. And the worst that can happen is that I end up giving you private lessons. Alone. Think about it."

She felt her face flush at his scrutiny. "I told you—"

"I know what you told me, but I like a challenge. Tell me something. Was your ex-husband a gentleman?"

"How do you know he's an ex-husband? For all you know I could be married."

"Even if you were, I'd still want you. But to answer your question, I asked around. It might interest you to know that the consensus around Seal Beach is that you're a professional divorcée."

"What's that supposed to mean?" she demanded.

"Have you ever heard of the term 'professional virgin'?"

She nodded.

"Think about it."

"If it means I'm going to stay divorced, it's right."

"That suits me perfectly."

"It suits me perfectly, too!"

He gave her a knowing smile. "If you say that one more time, it's going to begin to sound like overkill."

Ariel bit her lip in annoyance.

"You still haven't answered my question, Ariel. Was your ex a gentleman?"

She nodded.

"I'm not." He stood looking at her while the words sunk in.

There was a long moment when their eyes locked, and then he reached out for her and pulled her to him, one hand around her waist and the other hand tipping her face up so that her lips met his. She watched as his eyes closed, then unsuccessfully fought against the inclination to do the same. For no discernible reason she suddenly felt like giving in to him, just closing her eyes and letting her body melt against his. His mouth was demanding, slowly forcing hers open, and she could feel the roughness of his jacket where her breasts, thinly covered in the T-shirt, were being pressed against it. Well-remembered passions were beginning to flood through her body, and it was all she could do not to give in to the moment and return his kisses. But then, as suddenly as it had begun, it stopped, and he was once again standing back from her.

"All right, let's analyze what we have here," he said softly. "True, you didn't return my kiss, and true, you didn't exactly fall in my arms, but the feeling was there, wasn't it? And there's no use denying it, because you can damn well tell when the feeling's mutual."

A wary watchfulness was in her dark eyes. "Did it ever occur to you, Scott, that maybe your ego won't permit you to think that it wasn't mutual?"

He looked surprised. "Do you think I make a habit of forcing my attentions on uninterested ladies?"

She hated the word "lady." Now he was making her sound old enough to be his mother. "I really don't think I encouraged you. If I did in any way, it was unintentional, believe me."

"I'm not talking about encouragement," he returned. "No, you're certainly anything but encouraging. I'm talking about feelings, mutual attraction, chemistry, whatever. If you're telling yourself it's not there, then you're lying to yourself. Look, I make you nervous, don't I?"

She gave a reluctant nod.

"Do all your male customers make you nervous? Think about it. Do men in general make you nervous or is it just me? And if it is just me, do you know why I do?"

"Look, Scott, I really don't want to think about it."

"Oh, I can see that, all right. But I'm going to force you to think about it, Ariel. And while we're at it, let's get something straight. I'm not your ex. I'm not looking for a wife and a house in the suburbs and 2.4 children. I just want you, do you understand? I want you. And unless I'm very much mistaken about what that sexy little body of yours is feeling, this desire is mutual. So now's the time to run, Ariel, if that's what you really want."

She shrank away as he moved out from the wall, but he walked past her toward the door.

"Unfortunately, there's something else I have to do tonight," he said to her, "but I'll be seeing you, Ariel."

She was still standing there moments after he had left. Only a curious pedestrian who saw the lights on in the shop and came in to browse finally brought her back to reality with a jolt. After the woman left, Ariel locked the door to the shop and went into the back room to finish the fitting.

Ariel longed to call Sutton and ask her for some fresh advice, but she knew Sutton had a date. Instead, she worked slowly and carefully on the custom framing. She forcibly drained her mind of any thoughts of Scott, knowing that if she thought of him now, the fitting would suffer as a result.

It was after two in the morning when she finally finished, but the frames all fitted the art perfectly and she felt proud of her work. She had gotten quite attached to the graphics while working on them, already having developed favorites among them. They looked even better framed, very professional, and she wondered what price Scott would put on them. She wouldn't mind having one hanging in her living room. Perhaps he would be willing to make a trade of one for some custom framing.

On the other hand, maybe she didn't need anything reminding her of him every time she looked at her living-room wall. Maybe if they did indeed become friends she'd mention the subject to him. She had traded pictures with the other artists at the art show. Not that he'd make a trade with her. At least not for one of her "Rose Saunders specials," but he had expressed a liking for her foggy graveyard scene.

It was late and she was tired and she'd think about it later. She went upstairs, checked on the girls, then called it a night.

It seemed like only minutes later that she was abruptly awakened by a pounding on the apartment door. Staggering up from her bed, she glanced at the alarm clock and saw that it was only seven. She opened the door quickly before the pounding could continue, only to slam it in alarm when she saw Scott standing there.

"Hey, open up," he shouted through the door.

"Go away," she hissed.

"I swear I'm not here for any ulterior motives. I need to pick up my graphics."

"At seven o'clock in the morning?"

"I meant to tell you last night, but in the, uh, confusion, I forgot. I swear I'm not after your body—not this time, anyway."

She decided her neighbors, and maybe her daughters, had heard quite enough. Cautiously opening the door, she said, "If I give you the keys to the shop, can you get them yourself? They're right on the fitting table."

"Sure. A friend drove me over—I'll just load them in the car and bring the keys back up to you." His eyes left her face and began to move down her body.

Suddenly mindful of what she was wearing, she slammed the door in his face again.

"Hey, what's the matter?"

"I'll put the keys through the mail slot."

She found her key ring and dropped it through the door. Then, knowing she'd never get back to sleep, she went into the bathroom, threw some cold water on her face, and then got into some clothes. Deciding to go down to the shop in case he needed some help, she went to the door, but he had already returned and the keys were lying on the floor.

He had certainly been in a hurry to leave, she thought ruefully, then wondered who the friend was who had so conveniently been around at seven in the morning to drive him over. *Jealous of a man you don't want to go out with?* Ariel asked herself. Not really, she thought. Just a little jealous of other people who didn't always wake up alone. Mornings had always been her husband's favorite time to make love, and sometimes in the mornings still, before she was fully awake, she found herself turning over to the other side of the bed in expectation. An expectation that was never satisfied now.

She got back out of her clothes and went into the bathroom to take a shower. Taking a good look at herself in the bathroom mirror, she had to admit that she looked a lot different in the morning at thirty-eight than she had at eighteen. There was one thing to be said for older men: They would look just as bad the morning after. She would have to ask Sutton how she dealt with that.

The beach town never came fully awake in the summer until noon. It was generally overcast in the mornings, the sun burning the fog away around midday when the beachgoers and occasional tourists began to appear. The girls were still sleeping when she let herself out the door and walked to the end of the alley, circling back around and heading for Sutton's shop. Seeing a light in the back, she knocked loudly, and soon Sutton was unlocking the door and letting her inside.

"You want to go over to the Shoe for breakfast?" Ariel asked her.

"Good idea. I'm a little hung over and could use something, although I'm not sure what yet."

They walked to the corner and crossed Pacific Coast Highway to the small shopping center on the other side. The Wooden Shoe was the only twenty-four-hour coffee shop in the area and the favorite breakfast place for residents. Its decor left a lot to be desired, but the food was plentiful, and it was cheap.

The waitress brought their coffee immediately, and they both ordered hash browns and eggs and English muffins. Ariel was surreptitiously studying her friend's face to see if Sutton looked as bad in the morning as she did, but she couldn't see any difference.

"How do you do it?" she finally asked.

"Do what?"

"Look so good in the morning. I know you haven't had a facelift. Not that you need it," she hastened to add.

"You know I'm into yoga."

"So what?"

"So I stand on my head when I get up in the morning," Sutton explained calmly. "It's supposed to reverse the pull of gravity."

"What would you look like if you didn't stand on your head?"

"I don't know—I've been doing it for years. And why are you suddenly worried about how you look in the morning? It couldn't be Scott Campbell, could it?"

"I saw him again."

"Last night?"

Ariel nodded.

"You knew he'd be back."

"Well, sure, he left his graphics with me to frame," Ariel pointed out.

"That's not the only reason."

"It could be."

"And it could be he left them with you in order to have an excuse to see you again," Sutton said shrewdly.

"He looks so good, Sutton," Ariel sighed.

"Would you feel more comfortable with an ugly man?"

"I'd feel more comfortable if he didn't look better than I do."

"You look damn good for your age," Sutton told her emphatically.

"Yes, but so does he, and he's younger."

"So what happened? Are you going out with him?"

"No, but he kissed me."

"I think I'm in the wrong business," Sutton complained. "Nothing romantic ever happens to me in my shop."

"That's because your customers are all women."

"Not entirely. Lately I've been getting a few transvestites."

"No kidding?"

Sutton looked amused. "You know our mailman?"

"The young guy with the ponytail?"

Sutton nodded. "He started hanging around, talking to me, you know? I figured he was interested."

"And he wasn't?"

"He finally broke down and admitted the other day that he wanted to try on one of my dresses."

"Did you let him?"

"Sure. He looked good in it, too. Now some of his other friends are dropping by. I guess they figure I'm discreet."

"So what am I going to do about Scott?"

"What do you want to do about him?" Sutton returned.

"I don't know."

"What did you want to do about him when he was kissing you?"

"I wanted him."

"So what's the problem? Have an affair with him."

"My kids would have a fit," Ariel protested.

"So let them. Their father dates, why shouldn't you?"

"They give him a hard time about it, too."

"Ariel, they'll get used to it," Sutton counseled. "I

don't see why you think you have to be the only divorced mother around who lives like a nun. Kids never like it at first, but you've got your own life to lead."

"I wouldn't even know how to go about it," Ariel wailed.

"You just let things progress naturally."

"I couldn't even bring him home."

"So you go to his place."

"I don't know." Ariel paused. "The whole thing seems like more trouble than it'd be worth. I'd be causing dissension with my kids, and knowing me, I'd probably get emotionally involved. I don't really feel like going through that again. And when it ended, I'd probably be left feeling really stupid."

"You've got to learn to take it less seriously than you did when you were young."

"I'm just not sure I can do that."

"You won't know until you've tried," Sutton said.

Ariel looked at her watch and signaled the waitress for a second cup of coffee. They had about ten minutes before it was time to open their shops. She still didn't know what to do about Scott, but she had a feeling that following her own inclination was safer than taking her friend's advice.

"The thing about younger men," Sutton was saying, "is that you don't have to take them seriously. You just have fun with them, Ariel. But the fun can be terrific."

"Don't you ever get serious about them?"

"What's the point? These guys will eventually settle down and get married and have their own families. It's certainly not going to be with me. Even if I wanted to, I'm not about to start another family at my age. Anyway, it's safer than dating guys our age."

"Safer?"

"Sure. Guys our age want to get married again," Sutton pointed out. "They've usually been married once and see the advantages. Most divorced men get remarried within the first year."

"What about the women?"

"Not nearly so fast—if ever."

"That could be because of a lack of opportunity. Most men our age marry younger women the second time."

"I think it used to be for that reason, but not anymore. None of the divorced women I know want to get married again. Like us, they're enjoying their freedom too much."

"I can't say I blame the men," said Ariel. "I wouldn't mind having a wife. If I could just run the shop and not have to worry about anything else, it would be pure heaven."

"Amen to that!"

"Scott says it's the kiss of death to an artist."

"Being married?"

Ariel nodded.

"Well then, he sounds just right for you. And you've got art in common, which is a real plus."

Ariel laughed. "On the contrary, that's what we argue about."

Sutton opened her purse. "I'd like to stick around and discuss this with you more, but we've got to get to work. I just hope today's busy, because the beginning of the week was lousy."

Back at the shop Ariel found Jody up, dressed and waiting impatiently.

"Where've you been?"

"I had breakfast at the Shoe with Sutton."

"What am I supposed to eat?"

"There's cereal and bananas up in the apartment, Jody," Ariel said patiently.

"Why can't I go to the Shoe?"

Ariel took some money out of the cash box and handed it to her. "Go ahead, but I want you to have orange juice and not a Coke."

Jody looked thrilled at the prospect of going out to breakfast by herself. "Thanks, Mom. I'll see you later."

Ariel was kept surprisingly busy by customers all day. The most surprising aspect was the amount of people she signed up for Scott's workshops. Most of them were women, and she got the feeling they had seen Scott around and wanted to get to know him more than they wanted to learn how to paint, but she gladly signed them up, nonetheless. By the end of the day she needed only two more to fill the class, and she'd had several people who wanted a later workshop.

She began to think that there was no reason why she couldn't start teaching a class of her own. She couldn't as yet presume to teach adults, but she should be able to manage a beginning children's class. And she ought to start it now, while the kids were still on summer vacation. Maybe Scott would make a sign for her to put in the window. At the rate she was going, that display window would soon be filled with signs.

She'd half expected him to come around during the day, but he still hadn't appeared by the time she closed. She wanted to tell him the good news, but it would have to wait until Monday.

Nicole had a date that night, but Jody stayed home

and helped Ariel tie her display stands to the rack on top of her Volkswagen, and then load her paintings into the small car. Sunday meant another art show in a shopping mall somewhere, and she'd drop the girls off at their father's place early in the morning.

Jack occasionally dropped by to see his daughters during the week, but it was mostly on Sunday that he saw them. Sometimes Nicole protested the Sundays, particularly when her friends had special plans, but for the most part she and Jody seemed to enjoy their father more now than when he had lived with them. Which wasn't hard to understand, since now he devoted a whole day to entertaining them instead of watching ball games all day on television, as he had done when he and Ariel were married.

After eighteen years of being a dentist, Jack had chucked it all and gone into business for himself, importing catamarans and giving sailing classes in nearby Belmont Shore.

"Do you know what profession has the highest rate of suicide?" he'd yelled at Ariel shortly after telling her of his plans.

"It's dentists, that's who," he'd gone on, "and I'm beginning to see why. Everyone hates going to the dentist, and sooner or later they come to hate the dentist. I can't take it anymore, I really can't. Anyway, eighteen years of looking into other people's mouths is quite enough."

What he hadn't said outright but had certainly implied was that sixteen years of her had been enough, too. She shouldn't have been surprised; it had certainly happened to enough of their friends. She had known they were in a rut, that their marriage had lost all its earlier excitement, that they rarely talked about anything but the house and the children. But she had thought that was all part of marriage, that it was bound to be that way. During the last years of their marriage she had often longed for a different life, too, but she most likely would never have done anything about it.

Jack, whom she had always felt was the weaker partner in their marriage, had turned out to be the one with enough guts to end it. And, understanding the reasons, she didn't have the heart to even put up an argument.

So now she was living in a small apartment with the girls, Jack was sharing a house in Belmont Shore with three other men, and they both seemed happier without all the outer accoutrements of success they had collected over the years—items they had bought in part, she thought, to compensate for any real depth in their marriage. She had thought she loved their house and all their possessions, but it had felt as if a weight had been lifted off her back when most of it was sold.

Unlike Jack, she had been brought up to appreciate the things in life you couldn't buy, and now she hoped it wasn't too late to instill that in her daughters. At the very least, it was worth a try.

It was perhaps too late for Nicole, whose major concerns in life were her clothes and the kind of car her boyfriend drove, but Ariel couldn't really expect her to be different from her peers. She also had a keen intelligence and, at the moment, at least, was planning on being a physicist.

Jody was more like Ariel. She had shown a talent for drawing at an early age, which Ariel encouraged now that Jack was not around to belittle it. She also shared

Ariel's love of books and lately, although the visible manifestations of it got tiring, an interest in third world countries and world economics. That she now saw herself as a budding revolutionary without a revolution was beside the point. She really cared, and Ariel found that exciting.

The girls needed her now and she felt they really needed her undivided attention. An interest in a man would divert that attention from them at the time they needed it most. In a few years, when they were grown, then she could begin to think about a life of her own. And maybe then she'd be ready for it.

Chapter Four

On Sundays in Southern California the shopping malls are filled with art shows, and for the last five years Ariel had been a member of one of the groups that traveled around to the different malls. When she was married Jack had never approved, but after she had pointed out to him that she never saw him on Sundays anyway, at least not during baseball or football seasons, he'd given in. What he didn't dare vocalize was that he liked her around to provide snacks at halftime and bring beer when he ran out.

Also, when she was married the paintings she'd displayed had been far different. Then she had considered herself a serious painter, much as Scott felt now, but as a serious painter she'd seldom sold a painting. Her pictures had drawn a lot of interest then, but now they drew buyers. Thanks to Rose her florals now sold quite well, and if they weren't as satisfying to paint, the money they brought in was very satisfying indeed.

Ariel had never admitted it out loud, but Sundays were her favorite day of the week. She had never really minded being a wife, and even now she never complained about household chores. She adored her daughters and found from the first that motherhood was something that came naturally to her. She was even finding herself fascinated by the business aspects of her shop. But what completely satisfied her soul and made her most happy was being around other artists and discussing her craft, and Sundays satisfied that craving.

Painting was something she felt driven to do. When she was a child it had been encouraged, and her father had spent long hours teaching her first to draw and then to paint. Once married, however, all that had changed. Her husband put up with it as a hobby, understanding that housewives had to have something to do besides just tend to the house. And later, albeit reluctantly, he had allowed her to join an art show that took her out of the house on Sundays. But he never offered her a word of encouragement, never praised her work, and always, when given the opening, belittled her interest. At first she loved him too much to protest. Later she merely accepted it as part of married life. But her unswerving devotion to her painting had never faltered.

But while the act of painting itself was infinitely satisfying, it was a lonely profession, carried out in a void. The kind of input she received from the other painters on the show was what she had craved for years without even knowing it. She delighted in their talk of methods and use of color and by what process they had achieved a certain aspect to their painting. Painting alone all week was pure pleasure, once she had this camaraderie on Sundays. Even though it now meant she didn't get a day off from work all week, and even though she could just as well have tried selling her paintings out of the shop, Ariel still needed this kinship with other painters and never minded the ungodly hour she had to get up on Sundays to do so.

She dropped the girls off at their father's house and then drove on to Lakewood Mall. She parked as close to the entrance as possible and then began to unload the A-framed pegboards from the top of her car. She carried them inside two at a time and set them up beside Pat's spot, then went out and began to bring in her paintings.

Everyone on the show had their own specialty and they didn't infringe on those of others. Pat painted seascapes, and she was the star of the show. Her seascapes were ten cuts above those of seascape painters on other shows, and she had customers who drove from miles around to see her new offerings each week. Mary did missions, with an occasional Mexican village thrown in. Diana, the youngest member of the group at twenty-one, did three-dimensional acrylic paintings of Don Quixote. Gloria did wonderful paintings of jungle animals that looked real to the touch. Don did desert paintings, Alex did watercolors beautifully framed, and Marge did scenes of cities. George did pen and ink sketches and also sketched caricatures of customers. The florals were Ariel's domain.

When she didn't need additional paintings for the show she tried other things, and Rose occasionally had them do something different in class. But for the most part Ariel was satisfied with florals for the moment. Her technique was improving all the time, and she learned things about painting flowers with each new painting. And, of course, there was also the fact that they sold quite well, and every dollar helped in the raising of her two daughters. If mostly old ladies bought them, and if most of them wanted the paintings in colors to match their new slipcovers or the curtains in their bedroom, she didn't mind. She was bringing pleasure to them and in return was learning more about painting with each attempt.

Ariel hung her paintings, positioning them artfully against the pegboards she had painted white. They were all simply framed in unfinished wood strips, the cheapest kind of custom framing Windflower had, but she liked the way they looked. When she was finished, she took her folding chair and set it up next to Pat. Pat was English and had once been a bit player in films, but her first love had always been painting seascapes. She had offered to give Ariel private lessons, but Ariel was still too in awe of the ocean to even attempt to paint it.

Despite the crowds of shoppers at the mall for the August white sales, not many people were looking at paintings that day. Ariel sold two small florals for $75 each, which she considered well worth her time, but most of the other painters were grumbling about sales when it was time to go home. Ariel was both exhausted and exhilarated by the long hours and good talk, and she hoped her ex-husband wouldn't want to get into some long discussion with her when she arrived to pick up the girls.

Luck was with her, as Nicole and Jody were waiting out in front of the house when she arrived.

"Dad had a date and we told him to go ahead," said Jody, climbing into the car. With the paintings in the back they all had to get in the front, which was a tight squeeze.

"You should see his new girlfriend," drawled Nicole, giving her mother an arch look.

Practically every week Ariel was treated to a description of yet another girl friend.

"She's pretty weird," offered Jody.

Nicole disagreed. "She's not weird at all; I thought she was extremely chic."

"What does that mean?" Jody asked her sister.

"It means she has a punk haircut and wears Norma Kamali clothes." She was looking at Jody but her words seemed aimed at Ariel.

"Then she must be six feet tall," observed Ariel.

"Almost," said Nicole.

Ariel felt a sudden flash of envy. Not on her ex's behalf, but because she was so short she'd never been able to wear most designer clothing, and she deeply admired Kamali's designs even though these days she couldn't afford them.

"She's real young, Mom," said Jody, a look of disgust on her face.

"So what else is new?" said Ariel. Jack hadn't dated anyone over thirty since he and Ariel had divorced.

"She's twenty-two and just got her degree in engineering," said Nicole.

An engineer with a punk haircut? Ariel decided she'd let that one pass.

"Did you make much money, Mom?" asked Jody, and Ariel knew what was coming.

"Enough to stop at Jack In The Box on the way home," she told them. Hamburgers were always a sure way to keep them happy. For that matter, she liked them pretty well herself.

She parked in the garage behind the shop, and the girls helped her unload the car and carry her art equipment into the gallery before crossing the alley and going up a block to the Jack In The Box. The place was filled, even at ten o'clock at night, and they decided to get the food to go and eat back at the apartment.

Sitting on the stairs to the apartment and blocking their way was Scott. Wearing jeans and a dark blue T-shirt, she only saw his blond head at first in the dark. Why now? *Why when the girls are with me?* she found herself thinking. She knew she wouldn't hear the end of this from Nicole. Their father could have a twenty-two-year-old girl friend, and they'd accept that, but she didn't think they'd be so broadminded when it came to her.

"Where've you been all day?" were his first words.

Jody was standing back, giving him the once-over, and Nicole, Ariel saw with amusement, was assuming a languid pose. Actually, this might be pretty interesting.

"Lakewood Mall," she told him shortly.

"Shopping?"

"Mom goes out on art shows on Sundays," said Nicole, emphasizing the word "mom" in case he wasn't aware already that she was a grown woman with daughters. It was so obvious that Ariel found herself smiling.

He was still sitting there, blocking their way, and out of politeness more than anything else she invited him upstairs for coffee. She half expected him to refuse, but instead he got up and led the way up the stairs.

"Why's he coming up?" Jody hissed at her from the rear.

"Don't be rude, Jody," Ariel whispered back.

"Scott, this is Jody and Nicole," she said, introducing them as she turned on the lights in the living room. Jody was looking him over with suspicion. Nicole was simply looking him over, reminding Ariel of the vast difference between eleven and fifteen-almost-sixteen. "You girls can eat your burgers out on the balcony," she suggested.

"We'll eat in here with you," said Jody, and Ariel could see she wasn't going to be left alone for a minute. She seemed to have two built-in chaperones and wasn't sure whether this was good or bad.

She put water on for coffee and spread the food out on the table. "If I'd known you were here, I'd have gotten you a burger," she said to Scott, but he told her he'd already eaten.

The girls were being very quiet, their eyes going back and forth between her and Scott, which was beginning to make her nervous. Scott, conversely, seemed perfectly at ease, walking around the small living room and examining each item with interest.

"Scott's going to be teaching a class in the gallery," she said, and finally elicited a response from Jody.

"He's the one, isn't he?"

Not quite the response she would have hoped for, and she felt her face growing warm. "He's the one teaching the class, yes."

"He's the one who kissed you, isn't he?"

There might be something to be said for only having one child, she thought, knowing Nicole wouldn't have been so blunt. She looked over at Scott and saw he was trying not to laugh.

"Don't be gauche," said Nicole to her little sister.

"You mean don't be honest," said Jody.

"I've got some good news for you, Scott—the first workshop is almost filled already."

"You sound surprised."

"I must admit I was. It still seems like a lot of money to me."

"Are you going to have sex with my mother?"

All eyes turned to Jody. An earthquake couldn't have elicited a better reaction than had those words. Even Nicole looked nonplussed, and she was fairly blunt herself.

Ariel decided not to intervene. The question was directed to Scott and he could damn well answer it himself. After all, he was the one who had gotten her into this. If he hadn't made a pass at a middle-aged, divorced lady with kids, this never would have happened.

"Your son's pretty protective," he observed.

"That's my daughter," she answered. Scott blinked.

He was taking a closer look at Jody. Granted, the fatigues and combat boots looked more like boys' gear than girls', but the face beneath the olive drab helmet was feminine, wasn't it? She wondered how many other Seal Beach residents had taken Jody for a boy.

"It's all right," Jody was telling him. "I don't mind being mistaken for a boy."

"Why don't you take off that helmet and let me get a good look at you."

Jody reluctantly obliged, her sort, dark curls tumbling out around her face.

"I should have known," Scott said. "You're the image of your mother."

Maybe the hair. Maybe the eyes. But there was a vast difference between that small, unlined face and her own. It had been a lot of years since her face had had the youthfulness of Jody's, unfortunately.

Large, dark eyes were boring into Scott. "You still

haven't answered my question.'' The child never knew when to stop.

Nicole had stopped eating and was evidently waiting for the answer, too. Only Ariel started eating with quiet determination. This should teach him not to fool around with divorced mothers.

"By sex, do you mean am I going to kiss her again?"

"No. I mean real sex."

Scott looked at Ariel as though for help, but she ignored him. He could damn well get out of this himself. And he'd probably never come around again, either.

"What do you know about real sex?" Nicole's tone was scornful.

"I saw the movie at school."

"You mean you learned something from that?"

"I learned enough to know I'm never going to do it!"

"Well, if Mom hadn't done it, we wouldn't be here."

"Are you going to have another baby?" Jody asked her.

"Is that what's worrying you?" Ariel asked her.

"We don't have room for any more kids around here."

"I'm not going to have any more children, Jody."

"Promise?"

"I promise."

That seemed to satisfy her, but she could see that Nicole wasn't in the least pacified by that answer. Of course Nicole was aware you could have sex without babies.

"Be warned though, Jody—I'll probably try to kiss your mother again," said Scott.

"She won't let you," Jody told him. "And if I catch you trying, I'll kick you in the stomach." Then, having effectively put him in his place, she gave him a sweet smile. "Do you want to see my tent?"

As Ariel cleaned off the table, she could see Jody showing Scott not only her tent but the various army paraphernalia she'd been collecting in recent months. "What are you, a terrorist?" he asked her.

"No. I'm a revolutionary."

"She's waiting for Seal Beach to rise up against the rest of the country," Nicole told him.

The girls might not want her to date, but they seemed to be enjoying his company. She could tell Nicole was taken with his looks, and Jody always enjoyed a new audience. Next, Jody would be going into her tirade about the oppressed in Seal Beach. There weren't even any poor people in the area, but Jody was of the opinion that children were oppressed. Ariel could remember having the same thought at her age.

"Would you like a glass of wine, Scott?" she asked him.

"He's not staying, is he?" asked Jody.

"I want to talk to him about the class," she said firmly, not really caring whether the girls stayed up or went to bed. It had been a long day for all of them, but, unlike her, they could sleep late in the morning.

To her surprise the girls opted for bed, even closing the connecting door. Ariel was aware this wasn't to give her privacy, though, only themselves.

Scott had settled down again on the couch when Ariel brought out the bottle of wine and two glasses. With any other acquaintance she would have taken a seat beside him, but instead she moved one of the kitchen chairs to a position across from him and seated herself.

"That's a formidable defense you have in those two," he said with a grin.

"Sorry about that," she apologized. "They've never seen me with a man before."

"You haven't dated since your divorce?"

She shook her head.

"Why not?"

"Why should I?" she countered.

"I can think of several good reasons."

"That's several more than I can think of."

"Seriously, though," he began, "if I had realized that wanting you would involve so much—"

"You would have behaved differently?"

"Not at all. But I see I'm going to have to rethink my strategy."

"What were you doing here tonight, anyway?"

He was lighting a cigarette and looking around for an ashtray. She went into the kitchen and brought him back a saucer.

"You want to know the pretext I was going to use or my ulterior motive?" he asked.

"I'll settle for the pretext."

"Let's stop fencing—I was hoping to see you alone."

She looked around the room. "We're alone."

"Then why do I get the feeling there's a revolutionary with a rifle behind that door?"

"Probably because there is. But even if there wasn't, Scott, it wouldn't make any difference."

"Still lying to yourself, huh?"

Ariel shifted uncomfortably in the chair. She was glad the girls were home. Maybe she should keep one of them around her at all times. Not so much for protection from him, but for protection from herself. The appeal he had held for her when they first met didn't seem to be dying away, as she had hoped it would. Right now, it would be very nice just to walk over there and sit next to him on the couch. He'd put his arm around her and—

"Why don't you come sit over here?" he asked.

"I think maybe you'd better go, Scott. I was up very early this morning."

"What's this art show you were out on?"

"You know—one of those things in the shopping malls."

"You should keep the shop open on Sundays," he suggested. "Lots of people go to the beach on weekends. You'd probably do a good business."

She shook her head. "I like to talk to the other artists."

"What do you talk about? What decorator colors are in this week?"

"There are some very good artists on that show," Ariel retorted. "I learn something new from them every week."

"If they were real artists, Ariel, they wouldn't be sitting around shopping centers peddling their wares."

"They'd be sitting in their studios starving, right?"

"If they had any sense, they'd be sitting in their studios trying to learn to paint."

Her temper was rising. "Listen, Scott—with the exception of me, every one of those artists is totally supported by sales on that show. How many artists do you know who support themselves on their work?"

"Is that how you judge an artist? On how much money he makes?"

"I don't want to hear about how much money van Gogh made in his lifetime."

"Do you like his paintings?"

"Of course I like his paintings."

"But you would have preferred he'd turned out what everyone else of his time turned out, is that it? You would have liked him to organize a weekend art show and paint pretty pictures for people's living rooms."

"I see nothing wrong with trying to please people," she said coldly.

"You're trying to please the masses, Ariel. And the masses never have any taste."

"Then why do so many people have van Gogh prints in their homes?"

"That's now, not during his lifetime," Scott pointed out. "Now he's popular, and the masses always like what's popular."

"It's all very well for you to talk, Scott, but you don't have two daughters to support."

"Run right, your shop would support you, and you could use the rest of the time to paint something worthwhile."

"Your idea of worthwhile, I suppose."

"Come on, Ariel, I've seen what you can do. You don't have to paint that junk."

"Maybe I like that junk!"

"If I believed that for a moment, I wouldn't be here!"

"Are you telling me you like me for my artistic ability?"

"That enters into it. Mostly I like you for your mind."

"My mind?" she repeated in disbelief. "Everything I say you disagree with."

"Maybe I want to change your thinking."

"If that's what you have in mind, forget it. I've spent a lot of years formulating my ideas, and they're not going to change overnight."

"In other words, you're too old to learn anything new."

If she'd been sitting closer, she would have kicked him. If there was one thing she wasn't going to take from him, it was allusions to her age. She was well enough aware of the difference and didn't need him to remind her of it. "I don't think this conversation is getting us anywhere. It's late—"

"And you'd like me to leave," he finished.

"Yes."

"I thought you wanted to talk to me about the class," he reminded her.

"I already told you, a bunch of people signed up."

"So we start next Saturday?"

She nodded.

"You're going to sit in, aren't you?"

"I don't see how I can on Saturdays. Customers will be interrupting all the time."

"Teach Nicole how to do the custom framing. If she has any questions, you'll be there to answer them."

"If I can teach her by then, all right." Nicole enjoyed working in the shop and she shouldn't have any problem with the fractions involved. And Ariel enjoyed taking art classes—anyone's art classes. Come to think of it, she didn't even know what he painted.

"What do you specialize in?" she asked him.

"What?" He stared at her.

"What do you paint?"

"Anything I feel like painting. You'll find out next Saturday."

She stood up with a pointed look in his direction. "Well, I guess I'll see you next Saturday, then."

He remained seated. "You throwing me out?"

"I thought I was more subtle than that."

"Where do you sleep?"

"Where you're sitting."

He seemed to sink back into the couch. "Ever get lonely?"

"Try getting lonely with those two in there."

"That's not what I mean."

"Of course I do," she said, lowering her voice.

"Then why don't you do something about it?"

"Like fall into your arms?"

"For starters." He got up and walked over to where she was standing, backing her into the door.

"Why don't you find some nice young woman—"

"Nice young women are boring," he interrupted.

"For what you want, I don't see that it matters."

"Just what is it you think I want, Ariel?"

"You made it very clear what you want. Even if you hadn't, it's certainly obvious. Even my eleven-year-old knew."

His hand reached out and held the back of her neck, not moving, just spreading its warmth to her skin. It was a simple gesture, but it had more of an effect on her than just grabbing her would have. She stood very still, trying to stare him down.

A finger reached out to trace the outline of her lips,

then moved inside to trace the soft, wet underskin. She could feel her body stirring, moving almost impercepti- bly toward his. It was hard to understand why she was so aroused by his merest touch. Her eyes felt heavy and she fought a longing to close them, to shut out every- thing else and just concentrate on his touch. He was watching her carefully as though judging her reaction, then dropped his hands and reached for the doorknob.

"I think I'll wait for you to make the next move, Ariel."

"You might have a very long wait, Scott."

"And then again, I might not."

He opened the door and started down the stairs be- fore she could tell him not to hold his breath, that there was no way she was going to make the first move with any man. It hadn't been done that way when she grew up, and she guessed she was too old to change in that respect. There was no use kidding herself that she hadn't wanted him to make a move a moment ago, though. And he was probably well aware of it. If her girls hadn't been in the next room, she didn't think he would have suddenly acted in such a gentlemanly fash- ion either.

Well, if he was going to wait for her to make the next move, that solved her problem, anyway. She could just write off Scott Campbell as of right now.

She closed and locked the door, then made up her bed for the night. On the way to the bathroom she opened the door to the bedroom in order to get some cross ventilation.

"Did he kiss you, Mom?" came Nicole's soft voice.

"No, he did not!"

Soft laughter. "You sound disappointed."

"Go to sleep, Nicole."

"He's really very good-looking."

"And very young."

"You don't look all that old, Mom." Praise indeed from Nicole.

"We're just friends, honey."

"Oh, sure. Listen, I saw the way he was looking at you."

"I think you're imagining things."

"I'm not Jody, Mom. I know how a boy looks at you when he likes you."

"Good night, honey."

"And you were looking at him the same way."

"Good night, Nicole."

"Good night, Mom."

Chapter Five

Ariel wasn't positive until Scott showed up at nine-thirty the following Saturday morning that the work-shop was actually going to transpire. He'd stayed away from the gallery all week, and she hesitated to call him just to inform him that the class had been filled.

She had fitted the custom framing on Friday night, so that all Nicole would have to do would be to hand the jobs over to the customers when they came to the shop to pick them up. She'd also taught her daughter how to measure and take orders for custom framing, and Nicole was eager to make some extra spending money by working in the shop on Saturdays.

Ariel was just plugging in the 32-cup coffeepot when Scott arrived. The supplies he had requested had been delivered during the week, and Ariel cleared out a small bookcase she'd had in the apartment and brought it down to the store to display the paints, knives, and linseed oil in. She had affixed retail prices to them but decided to give the students the same artists' discount she was now giving on custom framing. The very large, square canvases were stacked against the wall.

Scott looked a little tired, as though he was not used to being up so early in the morning, and his paint-stained jeans and tank top mirrored her own. He put his paint box down next to the demonstration easel she'd placed in front of the class and grinned at her.

"Ready to learn how to paint?" he asked.

This early in the morning and already asking for an argument. "I'm ready to see what you have to teach that's worth $175," she retorted. When she didn't see him, she managed to forget how good he actually looked. No forgetting now, though, with him standing just inches away from her.

"Is that coffee made yet?"

"Not until the light goes on."

He nodded at her as their eyes met and held, and then he turned and began to put his paints out on his palette. When he bent at the waist, his tank top slid up, exposing a couple of inches of bare skin that had her wanting to reach out to touch it.

Well, she was a toucher, she reasoned as she carefully moved out of reach. She always loved touching her children's skin, feeling the texture, maybe offering comfort. Trying to clear her head of such thoughts, she concentrated on what he was doing. She'd never known a painter who limited himself to five colors before, and she was interested in seeing what effects he could achieve. She personally felt that raw sienna, raw umber, cadmium red light, cerulean blue and zinc white would be quite limiting, but she also liked the idea of the limitation, that it would be up to her to use those five to blend whatever shades she desired.

"Can't keep your eyes off me, can you?"

She came to with a start, realizing too late that she'd stopped watching the paint and started gazing instead on that strip of bare skin.

He straightened up and turned around, hooking his thumbs in the pockets of his jeans. "I thought maybe you were going to take me up on my offer and make the first move."

"That'll never happen."

"Oh, I wouldn't be so sure. I bet if I could get you alone for any length of time, I'd be able to wear you down."

She heard someone knocking at the front door to the shop and realized the door was still locked. Spared of having to make a suitable retort, she went to let in the first students, introducing them to Scott and telling them to sit anywhere. The others soon arrived, and before long Scott was explaining to them about his odd-sized canvases and large palette knife. None of them seemed to mind having to buy new supplies from her. She had thought they might complain about it, but perhaps people who could afford $175 workshops to begin with had money to burn. She knew she'd never feel she could afford a class that depended on such a large outlay of money.

She opened a package of Styrofoam cups and began to hand out coffee to everyone, while Scott took care of selling the supplies. Some of them even bought paint they didn't need when they learned about her discount to artists.

Nicole came down at ten, informed her mother that Jody was still sleeping, and then took her place in the storefront to wait on the few early-morning customers.

"This isn't going to be the kind of class you're used

to," Scott warned them as they were getting ready to start. "I'm not going to do a demonstration and then have you copy it, nor are we going to copy existing paintings. You're going to learn how to use your imagination here today, or at least that's what I'm hoping. I'll spend the first hour painting on my own, showing you a few techniques, demonstrating how I achieve color using only five tubes of paint. After that, I'll circulate among you and offer advice when it's needed."

It had been a long time since Ariel had painted anything out of her head, and she wondered if she could still do it. Judging by the reaction of the others they were wondering the same thing. Perplexed looks were being exchanged among the students, and she hoped there wouldn't be a sudden rush of dissatisfied customers trying to get their money back.

She watched along with the others as Scott took the top off a can of linseed oil and, holding his canvas horizontally, began to pour the contents directly onto the canvas. When he put the canvas back on the easel, some of the oil dripped off the white painting surface onto the floor. Ariel thought of the clean-up job she was going to have when the class was over. She was a neat painter herself, and seldom spilled anything. Nor had she ever seen linseed oil used in that way. Generally it was used to thin out paint when required.

Scott, speaking with the confidence and ease of an experienced teacher, told his class he was mixing a bit of raw umber with the cerulean blue in order to tone it down, then took a large glob of the mix on the flat of his knife and began applying it to the top of his canvas. Using long, smooth strokes, the canvas turned from white to blue.

Ariel sensed a restlessness in the class and looked around at the other students. The students were looking confused, and finally one of them spoke aloud. "What about the sketch, Scott?"

He turned to them smiling. "No sketches."

"You don't work from a sketch?" asked another.

He shook his head. "Not when I paint in oils."

"I don't think I can work without a sketch," one of them grumbled. Ariel was of the same opinion and was glad someone else had voiced it. Not having paid for the class, she didn't think she should be offering criticisms.

"Anyone else feel the same way?" Scott asked them.

Every hand was raised.

"Well, in my class you're not going to sketch. Outlines of any type are limiting to creative work. What they are, are restrictions you're laying down for yourself. In here, there are no restrictions."

"What about in portraits?" someone asked.

Scott grinned. "Let's just say I don't consider portraits creative work. They're a craft and seldom break any new ground. What I want you to do is let your minds soar, see where your imagination takes you. Put all preconceived notions out of your head, all mental pictures of where you think you're going, and just let your hand and your subconscious do the painting."

A few groans were heard.

"I take classes from Bill Yelland and we always copy pictures," one of the women spoke up.

Scott looked around at the class. "What about the rest of you? Do you copy pictures, or maybe photographs?"

Most of the hands were raised.

He shook his head in amiable disbelief. "I don't know about the rest of you, but I'm tired of seeing copies everywhere. I don't want to see any copies from you today; I want to see originals. This time you do the original and let someone else copy yours."

Somewhat daunted, the class subsided into silence and he continued his demonstration. Ariel found herself wondering whether her own subconscious would come up with anything. What would really be embarrassing would be if it came up with a picture of Scott. Twice that week she'd found herself absentmindedly sketching his face on the note pad she kept next to the telephone, and both times she had had to stop herself and destroy the evidence of her daydreams. All she needed would be to have one of her daughters tell Scott she drew pictures of his face when he wasn't around. And she hadn't done it consciously either time.

When Scott had a good half of his canvas covered with blue, he took some white paint on his knife and began to move it flat across the canvas, miraculously achieving the effect of clouds. Ariel had often used a knife when she wanted a somewhat three-dimensional effect, but Scott was spreading the paint thin, thinned down even more by the linseed oil on the canvas.

When he had requested large canvases and knives, she had thought they'd be consuming large quantities of paint, something she didn't think she could afford considering the price of paint these days, but if what he had done so far was any indication, his large painting was going to use far less paint than would a smaller one using Rose's techniques. She got an itch to try some of those clouds just watching him.

"I always wondered how he did his skies," Ariel could hear one of the women murmur, and several others agreed.

Never having seen one of Scott's skies, she didn't know what they were talking about. And where had they seen them? She couldn't remember ever seeing any of Scott's work around Seal Beach. It was always possible, though, that her father had hung some of Scott's paintings in his gallery. It was also possible he went out on art shows, just as she did, and neglected to mention it to her. Which, she thought, was the kind of sneaky thing he might do.

He started to paint in a deserted beach, a dilapidated wooden shack the only object in sight. She found herself just as interested in how the muscles in his back and shoulder and arm moved as he painted as she was in what he was painting, and she quickly turned her mind back to the subject.

Under the quick, deft strokes of his knife, weeds began to emerge from the sand, and pieces of driftwood came to life. With the merest flick of the blade, a few sandpipers were seen at the water's edge at the very bottom of the canvas. She was mesmerized now, unable to believe that someone could turn out a painting with such speed.

Somewhat impressionistic in style, it didn't look finished to Ariel when he finally stood to the side of the painting and set down his knife. She knew that Rose, and probably she herself, would have added additional detail, but Scott didn't appear to be a painter of details. She wondered if it said something about their respective personalities that she painted slowly and with great care, while Scott worked in the exact opposite manner.

If this was true, even without the age difference they no doubt wouldn't suit each other.

She saw that the class was moving toward the front of the room to get a better look at the painting, and she followed along. From close up it appeared even more unfinished, although she had to admit that she liked the look. Maybe there was something to be said for painting so fast. If she could get her speed up like that, she'd have no problem filling her display boards on the show. On the other hand, would people actually buy a picture like that? Most customers appeared to want photographic likenesses of the subject.

She noticed that even up close, the shack and the rest of the painting were done with very little paint, not piled on in the mode of most knife painters. She was beginning to get an itch to try it herself and only hoped she wouldn't make a mess of it and disgrace herself in front of him. It would be hard to continue to argue painting with him if it turned out he was the better painter. Not that she could have produced the *Banana Republic* suite that he had done, but she'd match the drawings of her children that she had sketched as they grew up against anything of his. Which reminded her that she hadn't done any in a while. It would be a shame not to capture Jody in her revolutionary phase before she outgrew it, and Nicole had grown up considerably since she had sketched her last.

She realized with a start that the rest of the class had returned to their easels and were busily squeezing their tubes of paint. Scott had been saying something to her, and she had to ask him to repeat it.

"I wanted to know what you thought."

"I don't know, Scott. I like it, of course, but I think

that like the other students I'd prefer to rough sketch first."

"You hate new challenges, don't you, Ariel?"

She didn't think that was true. Just running the store had been a new challenge, and she'd loved every minute of it. "Actually, I think it's going to be fun," she told him.

"I presume you're talking about the painting," he said, sotto voce.

"You presume right," she said to him before turning away, but not before she caught the amused glint in his sharp eyes. He had an artist's eye, all right—never missed a thing.

Willing her subconscious not to foul her up, she began to spread linseed oil all over her canvas, then hesitantly took up her knife. Just the size of the canvas seemed daunting. She squeezed more raw umber into the cerulean blue than he had, producing a darker blend; that suggested to her an overcast day, and she decided to go with that rather than cover what she'd already done. When she applied the zinc white onto the canvas instead of clouds forming, fog began to appear mysteriously, and she found that swirling the flat of the knife around on the canvas produced all kinds of foggy, stormy effects she'd never been able to achieve with such ease before.

Ariel glanced up to see how the other students were doing and saw that most of them, despite Scott's admonitions, were turning out replicas of his painting, and not very good replicas at that. He was right about one thing: it was far better to turn out an original than a poor copy. She caught his eyes on her and went back to her painting.

Her knife seemed automatically to reach for some raw umber, and then slowly a rock formation began to appear through the fog in the lower left portion of her canvas. She made the rocks smoothly with the knife rather than piling the paint on as thick as she usually did, giving the rocks the look of being fog-enshrouded; she began to get intrigued with the effect. The thick linseed oil layer on the canvas was even giving the scene a particularly glistening wet look.

She was totally immersed in her work when she sensed Scott's presence, and she looked around to see him standing behind her. She stopped painting. Being watched always made her nervous.

"I like what you're doing," he told her.

"It's fun using a knife."

"You'll find it frees you, too. You just can't do little, tight paintings when you're using it."

"Are you implying my paintings are tight?"

He placed a warm hand on her shoulder, and it seemed to warm her whole body. From the pressure on her shoulder she had a feeling he was aware that she was becoming flustered. "Don't take it so personally, Ariel. Anyone who uses small brushes ends up with tight paintings. I'd just like to see you get more free, that's all." At the word "free" the pressure on her shoulder increased, and she got the message that he was talking about more than painting. And she couldn't do a thing about it with some of the others watching.

To her embarrassment he called the other students over to view what she was doing. "I want you to take notice of how Ariel is painting. And keep in mind when you do so that this is a woman who usually paints small florals with a brush."

At the mention of small florals a couple of the women gave her glances of commiseration, and she remembered that one of them was the one who always painted from pictures.

"I don't think she's glanced up once to look at mine," Scott went on, "she's just letting her imagination loose and coming up with whatever seems naturally to take shape. That's what I want all of you to do. Maybe a cloud formation will suggest something to you, maybe the curve of a stroke. I don't care what it is as long as it's your own and not just what you saw me paint."

Scott dropped his hand from her shoulder and moved away. Somewhat chastened, the others returned to their easels and Ariel watched as some of them wiped off with a rag what they'd already painted. Well, they had plenty of time to start over again. The class went on all day and it wasn't even noon yet. Ariel figured at the rate she was going she could produce several paintings before the end of the day. That is, if she could afford to waste that many canvases.

She stood back from her painting in order to see what it looked like so far and found that the sky and the fog and the ocean were all parts of a whole, just the way the Pacific Ocean actually looked on the rare stormy days that Southern California got. She had always thought she'd have to go down to the ocean in order to paint it correctly, but that didn't seem to be the case. She knew her friend Pat at the art show did detailed drawings of the way waves broke before putting it on canvas, but Ariel began to think she could capture that just using her memory.

She continued working on the painting, adding as

one last detail a sea gull clinging tenaciously to the rocks. She had finished so quickly she felt she should keep painting and was starting to experiment by mixing some green when Scott came back.

"Leave it alone, its finished," he said to her.

"But it's not even noon yet," she protested.

"You've got to learn when a painting's complete. I hope you weren't planning on reworking it until the class ends. Get yourself another canvas and see what else you can come up with."

In other words he was telling her not to work it to death. Did she have a tendency to do that? She supposed she did. Her usual paintings looked just as real up close as they did from a distance, unlike Scott's. Well, it was his workshop, and she supposed she should do it his way.

Instead of getting a new canvas, though, she checked on the other students' progress, then slipped out the back door and went upstairs to see how Jody was doing. Still in pajamas, the girl was on the couch reading a book.

"Have you eaten, honey?"

"I had an orange."

"Jody, that's not enough for breakfast."

"Nicole used the last of the milk so I couldn't have any cereal."

"You want to run an errand for me?"

Jody didn't look thrilled at the prospect.

"I'm beginning to think I should feed the class some lunch, since it's going to be an awfully long day. Would you run down to Tony's and bring back some pizzas?"

The put-upon look disappeared. "Do I get some?"

"Of course."

"I'll be down in a few minutes," Jody promised, and Ariel went back downstairs to see how Nicole was coping in the front of the shop.

"I've made lots of money, Mom," she was told.

Ariel thought she was just referring to the orders of custom framing that people had picked up, but as it turned out, Nicole had also sold several new orders. Ariel checked over the calculations Nicole had made and couldn't find an error. She had made plenty of errors herself when she started the custom framing business but then, Nicole had had fractions in school a lot more recently than she had.

"I think I'll use you in here more often," she told her daughter.

"I wish you would. Otherwise, I'm going to be stuck with working at Jack In The Box if I want to make some money. They're the only place around that'll hire kids."

She thought of having Nicole keep the store open on Sundays, then dismissed the thought. That was the only day Jack got to be with the girls, and it wouldn't be fair. Anyway, she thought that Sundays were probably the time for browsers and not serious buyers.

When she told Scott she was sending out for pizza for the class, he offered to split the cost with her. "I should have thought of that myself," he told her.

When Jody came down Ariel gave her the money and ordered six, three large plain and three with everything on them.

"Why don't you get some beer to go with it?" Scott suggested.

"I don't think—" Ariel began.

"Yes!" roared the class, so she went across the street

to the liquor store and returned with two six-packs of cold beer. When the pizza arrived, she was glad she had. One beer each wasn't going to render anyone unable to paint, and it tasted just right with the steaming pizza.

She thought perhaps she'd sit next to Scott as they ate, but before she could make her move a group of admirers had gathered around him, all of them women, and one, she noted with annoyance, fed him an anchovy by hand. Talk about flirts, she thought to herself, going to the front of the shop to join her daughters for lunch. Well, if Scott was looking for a woman to date, he wouldn't have to look far. He already seemed to have a fan club among the students.

"I've already finished a painting if you want to take the afternoon off," she told Nicole.

"Oh, Mom—you said I could make some money."

"You'd rather work than go to the beach?"

"I can go to the beach anytime."

"What'd you paint?" asked Jody.

"Kind of a foggy ocean scene."

The girls wanted to see it, so she took them back to look. Nicole wasn't overly enthusiastic about it, but Jody pronounced it the best thing she'd ever done. Now if only Jody were an art critic....

"Could I take a class from him, Mom?" asked Jody.

"Well..."

"Please?"

"It's $175 a person, Jody."

"Is he making you pay?"

"No."

"Couldn't I take the one next week, then? Instead of you?"

"Jody, you've never worked in oils." Which wasn't a very good excuse, she thought, seeing the look of disappointment on Jody's face. "Look, what if I teach you what he's taught us? We can do it during the week."

Jody looked somewhat mollified. "You promise?"

"I promise. And then, when you've gotten the hang of working in oils, you can take one of the later workshops."

"Thanks, Mom."

The class was getting back to work, and Ariel decided to do one more painting during the afternoon session. She primed a canvas with linseed oil once more. This time the sky turned out a bright blue and the clouds, when she put them in, were drifting bits of pure white. An altogether more cheerful beginning than her last painting, and she found herself putting in green fields in the foreground with wild flowers coming into bloom. She stifled her tendency to make individual flowers, which would have been an impossibility anyway using the large knife, and she wasn't sure she'd achieved the effect she wanted until she stood a few feet back from the painting. From a distance the merest touches of color looked like flowers, and she was mentally congratulating herself when Scott came by to look.

"Couldn't resist doing flowers, could you?" he needled.

"I like flowers."

"I like them, too, when they're painted like that. Now, if you could get that effect when you do your florals...."

She had been thinking the same thing. The next time she started one of her bunches of flowers in a vase she was going to see what she could do with a knife instead of a brush. She wasn't sure about the vase—undoubtedly that would still have to be done with a brush—but the flowers and the leaves might look artfully casual done less intricately.

Scott was still standing there looking at her painting. "Could you do a vase with a knife?" she asked him.

"I can do anything with a knife."

She didn't believe that for a minute and told him so.

"Name something."

"A portrait."

"Portraits can be done with a knife. I'm not talking about photographic likenesses, you understand."

"You've done portraits with a knife?"

"I don't go in for portraits, but I could."

Well, if he could do a portrait with a knife, she certainly ought to be able to manage a vase. In fact, if he weren't watching her she'd try one right now.

Instead, she leaned both of her wet canvases against the wall and folded up her easel. Walking around to see how the others were doing, she saw that despite the fact some of them had persisted in doing a shack similar to Scott's, the students were all doing interesting paintings, and she felt they'd go home from the workshop satisfied with their work. They'd probably also recommend it to their friends. She began to envision Scott teaching workshops at her gallery forever. And the money she'd make from them would certainly go a long way toward solving her financial difficulties.

A couple of the students expressed an interest in taking another workshop from Scott when the session finally ended. One of them was the woman who had fed him the anchovy at lunch, and Ariel wondered about her motivation. She nonetheless signed them both up for the following Saturday.

Ariel joined the others in cleaning off her palette and found one huge advantage to having worked with a knife. All it took to clean the knife was one sweep with a towel instead of the endless soaking and cleaning that brushes required. A knife cost a lot less than a brush, too.

Some of the students began asking her about frames for their paintings, but when she mentioned custom framing, they soon lost interest. For herself, she thought wooden strips would look perfect around the paintings, but she knew most artists liked heavier, more ornate frames. The women on her art show all tended toward carved wooden frames with velvet liners. Some even went in for gold leaf. Now that she was making some money, she should probably frame a few of her own like that.

Scott must have overheard the students, because when the last one left he asked her why she didn't carry Mexican frames.

"I don't even know where to get them," she admitted.

"Look, could you keep the store closed on Monday?"

"What for?"

"I was thinking I could borrow a friend's van and take you down to Tijuana. I go to one of the factories down there for my own frames, and they're dirt cheap. You could've sold everyone in the class a frame if you'd had them on hand, and you'd do a good business with the other artists in the area as well."

Ariel was a little leery of a trip to Mexico with Scott.

An entire day alone with him in a van? It didn't really sound like such a good idea.

"I'll keep the store open for you Monday if you want to go," she heard Nicole saying.

"I don't know; what if something came up you couldn't handle on your own?"

"I'd just tell them to come back the next day. Go on, Mom, I can do it."

"I don't know whether I can afford—"

"With the profit you made today, we could practically fill up the van with frames," said Scott. "And that way you'll be making a profit on profits. Listen to me, kid, and I'll make you rich."

Magic words to Nicole. "Go on, Mom," she urged her mother.

"Well..."

"We can get an early start. I'll pick you up at seven, okay?"

Ariel found herself agreeing. She might as well make some extra money when she had the opportunity, and she'd also pick up some frames for herself. With elegant frames on her florals they would command a better price.

"I'd help you clean up, but I've got to get going," Scott told her.

She'd been hoping he would stick around, but she really didn't need any help in cleaning up. The students had all cleaned up their own areas, and all she would have to do was mop the floor.

It would have been nice to be able to discuss the workshop with him, she thought as she wrote him out a check for his share of the profits. On the other hand, it would give them something to talk about on the trip down to Mexico. It occurred to her as he took the check and started putting his paints away that he might want to go before she could change her mind. Actually, she was beginning to wonder how she'd been talked into it so easily.

"You've got a lot of talent," Scott said to her before leaving.

"Thanks."

"I'm serious. Some of those people here today were pretty good, but you were so far beyond them...."

"I had a good day, that's all."

"You could always have good days if you put your mind to it."

"And not paint like an old lady?"

His eyes gleamed. "Those were your words, not mine."

"Are you calling my mother an old lady?" came Nicole's voice from the front of the shop.

"That's your mother's assessment, not mine. I personally think she's got a few good years left."

Nicole's precipitous words and defense of her mother didn't fool Ariel one bit. Nicole was still reluctant to leave her mother alone with a man, and Ariel found herself smiling at the thought. And yet, she had offered to watch the store, thus freeing Ariel to go to Mexico with Scott on Monday. On the other hand, Nicole could very well be thinking that the more money her mother made, the more new clothes she'd be able to get for school in the fall.

"Why are you so eager for me to go to Mexico with Scott?" she asked Nicole after he had left.

"I'm not. I just want to make some money."

"You're sure you don't mind?"

"Mind what? Making money or you taking off with Mr. Wonderful?"

"Mr. *Wonderful*?"

"Listen, Mom, he's not bad. I'll bet a lot of women would love to go out with him."

"I'll bet a lot of women do go out with him."

"You should see some of the losers Carol's mother goes out with."

So that was it. If her mother had to go out, she wanted it to be with someone she could brag about. It was just no use trying to figure out kids.

"I'm really not interested in dating, Nicole."

"I don't know why not, Mom. Dad sure dates enough. And you're not that old, you know. You look a whole lot better than Carol's mother."

She had seen Carol's mother and it wasn't so much that Ariel looked younger but that she looked less harassed. Carol's mother had been left with five children, and Ariel didn't even know when she found the time to date.

The discussion was purely academic anyway. Since the day she met him when he had asked her out to dinner, Scott really hadn't asked her out again.

Chapter Six

Ariel borrowed a pink cotton sundress with spaghetti straps from Nicole to wear down to Mexico on Monday. What was an above-the-knee dress on Nicole hit Ariel below the knees, and with it she wore sandals with small heels.

She repeated her instructions to the girls so many times before she left that at the end they were just urging her to go. Not that they really needed all the instructions. Nicole would be sixteen in September and was quite capable of looking after her younger sister on her own. Ariel supposed it was guilt: guilt at looking forward so much to the trip.

When she looked out the back window at seven o'clock, there was Scott, sticking his head out of the driver's window of a beat-up white van with stylized daisies painted on the sides. She had a feeling that a van with painted designs was exactly the kind of vehicle the Mexican authorities were most leery of, and she hoped they wouldn't be subjected to a search going over the border and when they returned. But then, she felt sure that she and Scott looked like straight, law-abiding adults and not the kind of people who would be bringing drugs over the border.

"So you do have legs," was Scott's first remark as she climbed up into her side of the van and adjusted her skirt.

"Don't start on me this early in the morning."

"Haven't had your coffee yet?"

"I've had my coffee."

"Aren't you a morning person, Ariel?" he teased.

"Not two days in a row!"

He drove south on Pacific Coast Highway, then took a left at Seal Beach Boulevard, which would take him to the San Diego Freeway. Once on the freeway he asked her how the art show had gone.

"Very well. I sold four pictures, which means I can buy even more frames today." There had been a surprisingly large crowd at the Huntington Beach Mall, despite the fact it had been a perfect day to go to the beach. The show had grossed more than it had any other weekend that summer.

"Did you take your new ones out?"

She hadn't planned on doing so, but when she found they had dried quickly because of the thin application of paint, she had taken along the foggy one. She had displayed it but not priced it.

"I took the first one I did."

"And?"

"If you mean did I sell it, no. But then, I didn't have a price on it."

"Did you get any reaction?"

"I got a lot of good reactions from the other artists. The shoppers didn't pay much attention to it, though.

But then they're usually not looking for something that large."

"Or that well painted."

"Are you starting on me again?"

"Look, Ariel, I'm just trying to point out to you that a shopping mall isn't the place to find a crowd of art lovers."

"You'd be surprised how many people we get looking. And buying."

"I wouldn't be surprised at all. They're the same people you find at garage sales."

"Listen, Scott, even art lovers have to shop occasionally."

"I'm not disputing that. But when they're shopping for art, they don't head for the nearest mall."

Ariel looked out the window at the miles and miles of houses they were passing, all of them looking exactly alike except for the occasional backyard pool sparkling blue in the morning sunlight. She'd much prefer a few more hours' sleep to an argument with Scott.

"Are you listening to me?"

"Do you mind if I turn on the radio?"

"Ariel, I thought we could have some conversation."

"Your idea of conversation is a lecture."

He gave a belabored sigh. "This isn't my usual hour to be up and about, either. You could at least talk to me to keep me awake."

Ariel didn't know why the radio couldn't keep him awake, but since he was giving up his day to drive her down to Mexico, the least she could do was to make polite conversation. Except that it seldom remained polite with Scott.

"All right, Scott."

"All right, what?"

"All right, I'll talk to you."

"So talk."

She couldn't think of anything to say. Finally, she thought of something. "How long have you known my father?"

"Red? About ten years."

Well, that ended that line of conversation. "I thought the workshop was quite successful, didn't you?"

"Not bad. Some of those people will never do anything original, but I was really pleased with the others. If I made them at least think about being original, I accomplished something."

"Is there anything really original left to paint?"

"Of course there is. It's what the artist puts in it himself that makes it original. Have you ever taken a class where everyone sits outdoors and paints the same thing?"

"Morro Rock."

Scott laughed. "I think every artist on the West Coast has painted Morro Rock at one time or another. Okay, take Morro Rock as an example. When your class painted it, did they all turn out a little different?"

"They were all Morro Rock."

"You're being stubborn, Ariel. Tell me this: Wouldn't you rather see several different versions of the rock than only one version that everyone is meticulously copying?"

"I suppose so."

"Not only are they more interesting, but if you actually copy someone else's, it's plagiarism."

"I thought if you changed seven things—"

"Oh sure, that prevents a lawsuit, but in my opinion that still doesn't make the work original. I don't even think you should copy yourself."

Ariel, who did so frequently, kept quiet.

"It's not wrong, Ariel, I'm not saying that. It's just that you'll never learn anything that way. If you only copy what you've done before you never get around to extending yourself, to seeing what you're really capable of. Do you agree with me at all?"

"Sure I do—I just like to argue."

"No kidding," Scott said with emphasis.

"I used to be original."

"I'm sure you were. The trouble with getting older is that you tend to fall back on what you've done before; it's harder to try something new."

Ariel could do without references to getting older. Particularly from someone younger. "I think there comes a point when you have to be realistic."

"Meaning what?"

"Meaning I'm never going to be a great painter. Competent, maybe, but not great."

"What's your definition of great?"

"Picasso."

"What made him great in your opinion? His paintings, or the fact that he never stopped learning to do something new?"

"Both."

"I'd like to be like him. Still painting every day of his life right into his nineties."

Ariel didn't think she even wanted to be ninety. She was having a lot of trouble with just forty looming up not far in the distance. "Do you think he would've done as well as he did if he hadn't always had a wife around?"

"Meaning what?"

"Meaning you think marriage is the kiss of death to artists, but Picasso's wives made it possible for him to paint every day of his life. He never had to do anything else."

"Yeah, but you're talking about a different generation now. Self-sacrificing women like that aren't floating around these days."

"Thank God!"

Scott laughed. "You don't believe in self-sacrificing women?"

"I don't believe in anyone being self-sacrificing."

"You weren't a good little helpmate to your husband?"

"Let's leave my marriage out of this."

He looked over at her, which made her nervous. He appeared to be a good driver, but she'd prefer that he kept his eyes on the road.

"Was it too traumatic to talk about?"

"It wasn't traumatic at all. I just don't think it's any of your business."

"I'll tell you if you'll tell me."

"You've been divorced?"

"No."

"Then what are you going to tell me?"

He shrugged. "Anything you want to know."

She didn't think she was going to be able to keep up this running conversation for two hours. He also looked wide awake to her. She reached out to turn on the radio, but his hand closed over hers, preventing her from turning the dial.

"Come on, Ariel, tell me about your marriage."

"It's a pretty boring story, Scott."

"Bore me."

She gave him an exasperated look, but he was looking straight ahead and missed it. "We got married, we had two children, and we got divorced."

"Whose idea was the divorce?"

"His."

"Whose idea was the marriage?"

She had to think about that for a moment. "His."

"In other words, you let someone else decide all the important things in life for you."

Leave it to him to put that meaning on it, as though she were that easily led.

"Why did he want a divorce?"

"I don't know, Scott. I think it was some kind of midlife crisis."

"That could mean any number of things."

"It did mean any number of things. He wanted a different way of life, that's all. A different job, a different life-style...."

"A lot less responsibility."

She shrugged. There was that, too. But during the years when Jack had all the responsibility, he'd been very good at it.

"How'd you feel about the divorce?"

"Surprised. He was always the kind of person I thought enjoyed being in a rut. I didn't think he'd ever change."

"What else did you feel?"

"A little relieved. A little excited."

"Relieved about what and excited about what?"

"You taking notes on this, Scott?"

"I'm not asking you about your sex life, Ariel."

"That'll probably come next."

He chuckled. "Look, you can't say you were relieved

and excited and just leave it at that. If you do, I'm liable to put the wrong connotation on it."

She had never tried to express her feelings about the divorce to anyone before. She wasn't even sure she could. "I was relieved it was his idea. I was also relieved I wouldn't have to spend the rest of my life with him." Well, she had finally voiced those thoughts, and so far she hadn't been struck dead.

"Had you ever thought of ending the marriage?"

"Not exactly."

"What exactly, then?"

She sighed and slid down a little in her seat. "Every Sunday I used to read the real estate section."

"So what? I do that myself."

"I used to look for a place of my own. You see, I'd never had any say about where I lived. First my parents decided it for me, and then Jack. I wasn't thinking of leaving him, you understand—I just wanted some place that was all my own, where I could paint."

"He didn't want you to paint?"

"He didn't mind it as a hobby. He didn't like me to paint while he was at home, though."

"And so you didn't?"

She shook her head. "No, I did. But he didn't like it. I think he wanted to be my whole life—him and the girls—but they never were. There was always the painting, too, and he didn't understand that. I guess it was because he never cared about his own work that much."

"What'd he do?"

"He was a dentist."

"I hate dentists!"

Ariel laughed. "Everyone hates dentists. That's why

he finally got out of it." She saw a freeway exit flash by for San Clemente. Only halfway there. Another hour of talk, or rather questions, to endure from Scott. And later the long ride home.

"What did you mean when you said you were excited?"

"Change excites me. I liked the idea of starting over again, of doing things my way this time."

"Does it still excite you?"

She nodded happily.

"Would you ever get married again?"

"No."

"You didn't even have to think about it, huh?"

"I've had marriage, I've had my kids."

"Paid your dues, huh?"

"Something like that. Maybe it sounds selfish, but after the kids are grown I want to concentrate the rest of my life on me."

"That doesn't sound selfish at all, but don't you ever feel lonely?"

"Never."

"Yeah, but you're never alone."

"I'm never lonely when I'm by myself."

"Are you going to go the rest of your life without sex?"

So he finally got around to it. "Whether I do or not doesn't seem very important. Anyway, how do you know I'm going without sex?"

"If you'd been seeing men, your daughters wouldn't have reacted so strongly to me."

Scott didn't lack perception. What he also didn't lack was a one-track mind, and she wasn't about to get into a discussion of her sex life—or lack of one—with him.

She reached again for the radio, and this time he didn't stop her. She kept turning the dial until she found a station that played mellow rock, and when an old Beach Boys song came on she left it there. At least he didn't seem to have any more questions for the moment.

They were almost to San Diego when he pulled off the freeway to get gas. She made a trip to the ladies' room, then insisted on paying for the gas when she got back. He asked her if she wanted to stop to eat in San Diego, but she opted for Tijuana. She hadn't been down there since college, when groups of students used to go down for the bullfights, and she remembered the place with nostalgia. She thought of taking her daughters down sometime, but she wasn't sure how they'd react to seeing animals killed. For that matter, she wasn't sure how she'd react anymore.

"Did you go to college, Scott?"

He nodded. "Southern Cal. How about you?"

"UCLA." The two schools were rivals and she expected another argument, but this time he didn't bite. "Did you major in art?"

"No, I was pre-law at the time. How about you?"

"Languages."

"Languages? What'd you have in mind?"

"Traveling."

"And have you?"

"Not yet, but I will."

Scott started telling her about the past year he'd spent in Italy, and he was still describing all the places there she should see, when they got to the Mexican border. They were quickly waved through. Neither side of the border was worried about what was being taken into the country. It was what came out they worried about.

Little boys surrounded their van on the Mexican side of the border, where traffic was backed up. Some tried to wipe off the van with dirty rags, and others were selling everything from chewing gum to large, ceramic banks in the shape of bulls. Scott handed some change to one industrious boy before starting up again.

The Baja California authorities seemed to have cleaned up their act. Ariel could remember the miles of abandoned cars that had led into the town where the poorer people had lived with no sanitation facilities of any kind. Now that area had been cleaned up so as not to offend the tourists, but she had a feeling the poor were still living under the same conditions elsewhere. She thought that it was no wonder so many tried to cross the border illegally; there was simply not enough work to go around in this small section of Mexico.

Scott drove slowly through the downtown section of Tijuana and parked in the lot at the Jai Alai Café. Ariel got out of the van and stretched, feeling stiff after the hours of driving. The temperature was a good ten degrees warmer than it was in Seal Beach, and she was glad she'd dressed lightly.

He put his arm around her casually, resting his hand on her bare shoulder. "Come on—let's get something to eat."

The gesture, which would have disturbed her in Seal Beach, seemed quite acceptable in Mexico, and would in fact offer some protection from the men who always seemed to be lying in wait for female tourists. They headed down the crowded sidewalk past countless questionable bars, shops selling wrought silver, stores that featured hand-painted ceramics and colorful clothes, and past several restaurants before Scott led her into one. It was rather dim inside and somewhat cooler, although it didn't have air-conditioning.

A waiter with a mustache even larger than Scott's set a bottle of wine on their table as he passed.

Scott smiled at her and shrugged. "I guess we're going to have wine with our lunch." He uncorked the bottle himself and poured them each a glass.

When the waiter came back, it turned out they both wanted eggs. She ordered hers sunny-side up and Scott ordered his over easy, but the instructions were wasted. When they got their orders the eggs were scrambled, mixed with onions and green peppers. A spicy red sauce was liberally poured on top. Instead of toast they were served tortillas, and Ariel ended up making a sandwich of her eggs.

They finished the meal off with strong coffee and a glazed pastry each. "Is the factory far from here?" she asked him.

He nodded. "Outside of town. Not really so far, but it's annoying to get to."

Ariel gave him a quesitioning look.

"They put the factory out in the middle of nowhere without even an access road," Scott explained. "I think it was in an effort to hide from the government and thus avoid taxes, but that's only my guess. You'd never have found it on your own, though."

"How'd you find it?"

"A friend took me, and before that a friend took him. There's another factory across the border in the States, but their prices are considerably higher. And Hector will make up special sizes for us while we wait. I hope you remembered to bring your resale license."

She nodded.

"Good. Otherwise they'd tax you going across the border."

"I've always liked Tijuana," she told him as they headed back to the van.

"You're kidding. Nobody likes Tijuana."

"I do. I guess it's because it's the only foreign country I've ever been to."

"Have you been farther down?"

"Only as far as Ensenada."

"Well don't judge Mexico by border towns. La Paz is great; you should go there sometime."

She should go to a lot of places, but she couldn't afford it at the moment. "I guess my father'll be seeing most of it."

"Lucky man."

"Despite the kiss of death?"

He laughed. "Yeah, despite that."

They headed out of town and passed the bullring on the way. That was as far as she'd been before in the actual town, and while she saw some shacks perched on the hillside with an occasional goat grazing nearby, she also saw some modern apartment buildings that looked as though they were recent additions in the area. They all had a lot of wrought-iron work on them, but she'd heard that while they looked good on the outside, many of them had been built with no plumbing.

Sure enough, it wasn't long before Scott pulled off the dirt road and headed across a field. There were deep ruts filled with mud and high weeds, but the van made progress, albeit slowly, whereas her VW would have got stuck. They finally approached a low stucco structure, and he pulled up and parked.

"Does the factory have a name?"

"I don't think so—it's just Hector's place."

Scott led her directly to Hector Rodriguez's office, where she was introduced to an elegant-looking man not more than forty who immediately offered them each a glass of wine. Ariel was about to refuse it when she caught Scott's look of caution and instead nodded her thanks. The wine made her sleepy. At this rate she was going to need a siesta.

After the glasses of wine and polite conversation, Hector took them on a tour of the factory and then into the showroom, where he pointed out his samples to Ariel. There was every kind of frame she could possibly need, from modern strips to the more ornate gold-leafed models. And, as Scott had told her, the prices were dirt cheap. She'd been spending a lot more on custom framing her pictures with plain frames than she would have on much prettier frames. And florals looked good in pretty frames.

Hector took down her order as she pointed out the different frames she wanted, and then Scott put in an order for large square frames in walnut for both the workshop and himself.

"I used to make them myself," he told her, "but I can get them cheaper here. Which leaves me more time for painting, and I don't mind that."

Hector told them it would be a three-hour wait while the order was made up, and offered them his office while they waited. When Scott asked her if she'd like to drive to Rosarita Beach in the interim, she quickly agreed. The temperature in the frame factory was easily over a hundred degrees, and she felt in need of some fresh air to clear her head.

The seats on the van were burning hot after having

been parked in the sun, and Scott found an old blanket in the back of the van to set over them. "I like your friend Hector," she told him as they took off.

"He's great, isn't he? He's an artist, too—quite a good one. Plus, he designs all the frames."

"I loved the ones with the curved burlap liners."

"Your customers are going to love them, too."

Her mind was filled with visions of how her paintings would look out on the art show with her new frames. She was sure she'd sell twice as many paintings as a result.

They reached Rosarita Beach quickly. Scott parked in the lot of the hotel, then led her around the structure and down to the beach. He had brought along the blanket and spread it out a short distance from the other sunbathers. To her surprise, Ariel saw that most of the women were sunbathing topless.

"I didn't think that was allowed in Mexico."

"It's allowed anywhere these days where they want to attract tourists."

He didn't seem interested in viewing the pulchritude on display, so she relaxed a little. It was somewhat embarrassing to be surrounded by half-naked women when she was with a man she didn't know that well.

Scott removed his sport shirt and leaned back on his elbows. "We should have brought suits."

"At least it's cooler down here," she observed. "But then, it's always cooler near the ocean."

"Feel free to take off your dress if you want. No one will say anything."

"Forget it!"

"You a prude, Ariel?"

She had always thought she was just the opposite.

By herself she might have done just that, but she wasn't going to go out of her way to incite Scott to passion.

"You've got enough to look at, you don't need me, too."

"But you're the only one I want to look at."

She went so far as to pull her dress up to midthigh, but that was enough. The sundress left enough of her exposed. And if she wasn't careful, she was going to get a sunburn.

"Have you ever done any nude sunbathing?"

"I've never been anywhere where it's allowed." She didn't think she'd want to be, either. Even now she couldn't help glancing around, checking out the other women's bodies against her own. She knew her body still looked good, but it wasn't the body of an eighteen-year-old and never would be again.

The top of her sundress was elasticized, making the spaghetti straps merely decorative. She untied them and let them hang down so that if she did get a little suntan, she wouldn't have strap marks. Scott watched her closely, as though he expected her to remove the entire dress. Well, let him expect it, he'd just be disappointed. They were down here on a business trip, not for pleasure. She never should have accepted an invitation from him to go to the beach.

She lowered her body onto the blanket, making certain that she was as far away from him as possible. She was afraid that just an accidental brush against him might be misinterpreted.

"You've got a good body. I don't know what you're so modest about."

"For a thirty-eight-year-old."

"You sure seem to have a hang-up about your age. If you lived in Europe, you wouldn't feel that way."

"But I don't live in Europe. I live in southern California, the center of the youth culture of the world, in case you hadn't noticed."

"Which is conspiring to make you feel very old, is that it?" For once he didn't sound amused, only interested.

"I just don't see why everyone wants to look eighteen—perpetually. When I was eighteen, I could hardly wait to get older."

"Does your ex like young women?"

"Of course he does; he's a man."

"Not all men—"

"Don't tell me that! My father married a woman young enough to be his daughter. It's all around, Scott—open your eyes."

"Well, you know, when you get to a certain age, I guess there's a tendency to want to recapture your youth. Have a second chance. For that matter, a lot of older women are going out with younger men these days."

Ariel couldn't argue with that; Sutton was a prime example. But was he advocating it for her? Was he suggesting she be the older woman to his younger man? If so, he could just forget it. The last thing she needed was to be constantly reminded of her age. My God, the women she knew, notably some of those in Rose's art class, were already talking about getting plastic surgery performed on their faces, and they weren't any older than she was. Couldn't people be allowed to grow old gracefully anymore?

"Couldn't we change the subject, Scott?"

"Not until I make my point."

"Oh, there's a point to all this?"

"Of course there is. What did you think, I was just trying to soften you up?"

"That had occurred to me," she murmured.

"My point is, there are two kinds of men: those who go out with a woman for her body, and those who go out with a woman for her mind."

"And you're of the mind variety, I suppose."

"That was my point, yes."

"Good try, Scott."

"But you don't believe me."

"No." But even if she did, she wouldn't understand it. She liked his mind, too, but if he didn't have that terrific body to go along with it, she didn't think she'd be attracted. God, maybe she was turning into a dirty old lady!

Ariel rolled over on her stomach, turning her face away from him and resting it on her arms. The sun was warming her body to the point where external heat and internal heat seemed hard to differentiate. She had noticed this before, the ability of the sun to arouse her to a degree, and she should have remembered that before going to the beach with him. Whatever the reason for her heated body, she was uncomfortably aware of his half-clad body spread out beside her own.

"On the other hand..." Oh, no, he was going to start again.

"Scott?"

"Yes?"

"Why don't you just let me take a nap?"

"Yes, Mother. I'll just take my pail and shovel and go play in the sand quietly."

She chuckled. She had sounded motherly—conditioning, she guessed. Not that she felt motherly in the least toward him, and she certainly wasn't that much older that he should see her as a mother figure. That would really be humiliating.

She closed her eyes and let the soothing rhythm of the waves lull her. For two consecutive mornings she'd got up far too early, and she wasn't at an age anymore where she could do with so little sleep and not feel the effects of it. And there she was, thinking about age again! Was she becoming obsessed with the subject? She couldn't honestly remember even giving it much thought until Scott came into her life, but now she found herself thinking of it more and more. Was the rest of her life going to be like this? If she was this bad at thirty-eight, how was she going to be in her forties when Jody was finally grown?

It had been so much easier being married. Jack was older than she was, they had seemed to be aging at the same rate; she wouldn't have spent a moment's thought on any of this if they'd still been together. If only her body didn't tell her she still needed a man, when her mind had thought she was past all that. When did it stop, at forty? Fifty? Never? Despite the warmth, she felt herself shudder at the thought. Was she doomed to lust after men's bodies until her dotage? She'd really have to have a talk with Sutton about all this. Sutton always had all the answers.

She hadn't known she was asleep until Scott's hand on her shoulder, gently shaking her, caused her to wake up with a start.

"We'd better get going. It's four-thirty."

She sat up on the blanket and tied the straps to her dress. "I guess I really slept."

"Umm, mumbles and all."

"Mumbles?"

"You mumble in your sleep."

"What did I say?"

"You kept begging me to make love to you, but I didn't think there was enough privacy."

"Liar!" Ariel stood up and brushed the sand off her body, then followed him to the parking lot. She felt well-rested after her afternoon nap and thought she might adjust very easily to a place that had siestas in the afternoon.

True to his word, Hector had their frames all ready for them, and two of his men helped them load the van. The amount of money she parted with didn't seem great, compared with the quantity of frames she now possessed. A little arithmetic in her head told her the profits were going to be a delight.

Traffic crossing the border was backed up for a good mile. Ariel was anxious not to leave the kids alone too long, and when Scott had suggested dinner in Mexico before they left, she had demurred. A take-out place along the way would suffice.

She had always felt she was prepared to expect the unexpected, but found in reality that she wasn't at all prepared for the fiasco that occurred at customs. One of the officials informed them, in fluent English, that customs for resale merchandise closed down at six, and it was now six-fifteen. And since her invoice for the frames had to be stamped before they could cross the border with the frames, the van had to be confiscated for the night and could be picked up at nine in the morning.

Feeling helplessly frustrated, she glared at Scott. "Did you know about this?"

"If I had, I would've got us here earlier."

Ariel looked beseechingly at the customs official, to no avail. He merely told them to move their van out of the way, as they were holding up the border traffic.

"What are we going to do? Scott I've got to get home."

"I guess we can rent a car and drive back down in the morning."

Two trips to Mexico for one load of frames?

"Or we could go to a motel."

"I think you planned this!"

"Don't get paranoid, Ariel. I have things to do tonight myself."

"Yes, but you didn't leave two children all alone at home."

"Your daughters are both old enough to baby-sit—what's the problem?"

"How do I explain to them I'm spending the night in Mexico with you?"

"Oh, is that what's bothering you?"

Furious, she kicked a tire of the van and got nothing for her effort but a sore toe. A night in Tijuana alone with Scott. Great. Just great!

Chapter Seven

"What did she say?"

"*Mother,* does this mean you're spending the night with *Scott?*" Ariel did a creditable imitation of Nicole's voice.

He chuckled. "I've really ruined my image with them now."

"Your image and my reputation."

"Will they be all right alone?"

"Probably, but I think I'll call Jack and let him know the situation." And far better for him to hear it from her than perhaps getting a distorted version from his daughters.

She put more change in the pay phone and soon heard the voice of Jack coming to her as though through a tunnel.

"Where are you, Ariel. I can barely hear you."

"In Mexico, Jack." She almost had to shout to be heard. Scott was standing at some distance, but probably couldn't help overhearing.

"Mexico? What're you doing down there?"

She explained the situation to him, glossing over only the fact of whom she was with.

"Who'd you say you were down there with?"

"A friend of mine. An artist."

"Don't tell me it's the same one I heard about from the girls. The young guy?" Just what she needed, another reference to Scott's age. And from someone who reserved his dating for the very young.

Ariel made a noncommittal sound. "Could you check on the girls tonight?"

"I'll do better than that. I'll bring them over to stay with me tonight. You just have a good time—best thing in the world for you."

She hoped that didn't mean what she thought it meant. Was her ex-husband now concerning himself with her sex life too?

"We should be back around noon," she said before realizing that Jack had already hung up. She turned around and saw Scott grinning at her.

"So, did you get your ex's approval?"

"I think I got more than that. I have a feeling he was giving me his go-ahead." Perhaps Jack hadn't thought it was really a business trip.

"Great." His grin was stretching even wider. "Then let's take advantage of it."

"My ex-husband doesn't direct my life," she said, following him to the desk of the hotel where they had tentatively planned to get two rooms for the night.

Except during marriage, Ariel had never checked into a hotel with a man, and since neither she nor Scott had any luggage she thought there might be a problem. There was none, however, and the desk clerk even seemed surprised that they requested separate rooms. He did manage to put them on the same floor.

"Do you want to check out the rooms before we eat?" Scott asked her.

From the looks of the lobby, Ariel wasn't in any hurry to see the rest of it. And this was the best hotel in town. "No, let's eat first."

She felt some trepidation about how they were going to spend the time before she could reasonably expect to go to bed for the night. She knew there were only two choices in Tijuana: You could go to a small bar and get drunk, or you could go to one of the nightclubs with questionable floor shows and get drunk. Neither option appealed to her.

She felt he was making as much of an effort to stretch dinner out as she was, but it only takes so long to eat a steak and a salad, and when a line had formed outside the restaurant of people waiting for a table, they really couldn't justify dawdling over endless cups of coffee.

It was still light out and the shops were still open when they left the restaurant. They walked around trying to find the equivalent of a drugstore and finally found one on a side street, where they were able to purchase toothbrushes and toothpaste. On the same side street was a movie theater featuring a Fassbinder film she'd been wanting to see. She generally went to the movies with her daughters, and they invariably refused to see foreign films.

"Want to go to the movies?" she asked Scott, hoping he'd agree. It would at least kill two hours, and after that she could plead exhaustion.

From the way he looked at her she had a feeling he knew she was putting off their inevitable return to the hotel. "Why not?" he finally agreed.

She hadn't even thought about subtitles before they entered the theater, and of course they were in Spanish. German wasn't one of the languages she'd studied in college, but she could read the subtitles well enough. It was just that they didn't seem to bear any relationship to what was happening on the screen. It was a confusing two hours, spent in trying to figure out the correlation between the action and the purported dialogue, but at least it kept her awake in the small, crowded theater that lacked both air-conditioning and ventilation of any kind.

When they left the theater, they tried to figure out what the movie had been about. Scott had also been able to read the subtitles but seemed as confused as she was. It was something to discuss, though, and they continued the discussion in the hotel bar over a nightcap.

"Forget the movie," Scott said finally. "I think you're avoiding the subject."

Certainly she was avoiding the subject. And she was going to continue avoiding the subject.

They were seated at a small table in a dimly lit corner, and now he moved his chair over closer to hers. "Couldn't you just think of this as a romantic interlude? Something to seize and enjoy before returning to the more mundane business of tomorrow?"

"If you mean what I think you mean, forget it."

"You know exactly what I mean."

His leg moved over to brush against her own and she took a quick drink of her margarita. She knew it was potent when drunk that way, but at the moment she needed some potency. "I'm not looking for a romantic interlude, Scott."

"I know you weren't looking for one, but when one presents itself, why not take advantage of it?"

"I feel like I'm the one being taken advantage of."

"If you're suggesting I'm taking advantage of you,

then I suggest you take a closer look at the situation. We're both stuck here, and I'm no more pleased about it than you are. Nor am I any more at fault. That isn't to say that I wouldn't be pleased about it if things were going a little differently, of course."

"You mean if I were willing to share your room."

Scott took her hand and held it on his lap beneath the table. "I swear I think your daughter's got more sophistication than you do when it comes to men."

"Leave my daughters out of this!" She tried to snatch her hand out of his grasp, but he held it firmly.

"Gladly. I just wish you'd quit acting like a skittish virgin around me."

"Am I really that bad?"

"Let's just say your behavior isn't exactly the norm. Times have changed, Ariel."

"And people today are jumping into bed together right and left."

He let go of her hand and lit a cigarette. "And you're still looking for a six-month courtship first, is that it?"

"Not at all. I just don't think that casual sex is the answer in my position."

"What do you mean by your position? Are you referring here to the fact that you have two impressionable daughters?"

"I told you to leave my daughters out of this."

"But I don't think you're leaving them out of it. Tell me the truth. If you had no children, would you still feel the same way?"

Her first impulse was to say yes, but that wouldn't be the truth. The truth of the matter was, she did want her daughters' respect, and she was afraid she'd lose it if she behaved in a way that didn't conform to their ideas of how a mother should act. "I'm not sure. I never really thought about it."

"Your older daughter will probably assume we had sex down here whether we do or not. And your younger daughter, despite her questions to me, will probably asume we didn't. And in any case, no one would really know for sure."

"They'd know."

"What are they, mind readers?"

"I'd act differently."

"I think you're wrong, Ariel. People act differently when they fall in love, but I don't think they act differently after sex. Unless you think your guilt would be so great that it'd show. Is that it? Do you feel sex is something to feel guilty about?"

"No. I have no problems with that. What I do have a problem with is your tendency to analyze everything. I feel like I'm in a classroom, and your lecture is leading up to a demonstration."

"Believe me, I'm capable of leading up to it in much more romantic ways. I was trying to ease your mind, that's all."

"Well, you didn't ease my mind. All you managed to do was get me out of the mood."

"Now you tell me. I didn't even know you were in the mood." He gave a rueful shake of his head, then called over the waiter and ordered two more margaritas.

"I've had enough to drink," she told him.

"Since I failed, I thought maybe the drinks could get you back in the mood."

"I really don't want it, Scott. I think I want to go to bed now."

"Alone?"

"Alone."

She had expected an argument, but instead he called back the waiter and canceled the order. He stood up and threw some money down on the table, and in silence they headed for the antiquated elevator.

Ariel found herself feeling a bit as though she'd missed an opportunity. She was attracted to Scott and had enjoyed his company all day. She wished she were the kind of person who could just naturally follow him to his room and cap off a pleasant evening with some enjoyable sex. Only she had a strong gut feeling that she wasn't that kind of person, that for her an interlude of sex would evolve into something more, perhaps even something serious. She had no confidence in her ability to separate sex from an emotional involvement. Despite his obvious desire for them to have sex together, she was certain he wouldn't want to wake up in the morning and find that his casual sex partner of the night before was now viewing him as a love object instead of a sex object.

Maybe she'd find that she could handle it, but she wasn't going to take that chance. The last thing her daughters needed was a mother who was mooning over some young lover. The divorce hadn't been easy for them, and they needed stability in their lives at this point. And she needed an unfettered mind. Yet a certain part of her was still urging, "Go on, take the chance. You don't know until you've tried...."

They came to the door of her room first, and for a moment he stood in front of her, looking down into her eyes. She thought he'd kiss her then, but instead he seemed to be holding to his stricture of her having to make the first move. "I'll ask for a wake-up call," he said. "That is, if there's a phone in the room. About eight?"

"That'll be fine. See you in the morning then, Scott."

He simply nodded and continued down the hall. He waited until she was in her room, and she heard his own door close soon after.

She put on the overhead light in the stuffy room and immediately went over to open the door leading to a small balcony, which appeared to tilt away from the wall of the building. Several moths flew in and congregated around the unshaded single bulb up on the ceiling.

The room contained a sagging double bed and a wooden dresser scarred by countless cigarette burns. She didn't see a telephone, but she knew she'd wake up early in the morning, particularly since she was going to bed earlier than she usually did. She took off her dress and laid it across the top of the dresser, then went into the bathroom to get ready for bed.

There was a shower stall without a curtain, but the water was plentiful if tepid. The water for brushing her teeth was another matter. She simply thought the toothpaste tasted funny until she went to rinse out her mouth. The water was extremely salty with an unidentifiable taste, and she was thankful she hadn't swallowed any. What she and Scott should have done was purchased bottled water, but it was too late now.

She heard a noise and looked down in time to see a large water bug scurrying out of the bathroom. She grabbed one of her shoes and pursued it across the room, but it was too fast for her and disappeared into a large crack in the corner of the wall. Moths didn't bother her. Water bugs were a different matter, and Ariel only hoped it wouldn't return when she put out the light.

Gingerly lifting back the covers on the bed, she inspected the sheets for any more bugs. She went over to flick off the light switch, and out of the corner of her eye she saw something move on the wall. It's nothing, she told herself, you're just getting paranoid after the water bug. But she turned her head in time to see a lizard slide into the shadows. There was no way she could kill something as large as a lizard, even if she could catch it. But she also knew there was no way she could share a room with a lizard, either. She knew they were harmless, knew they were more afraid of her than she was of them—well, maybe she wasn't so sure about that—but none of that rationalization helped in the least. She also knew she'd lie awake all night waiting for an attack by the lizard. If it just fell off the ceiling and landed on her, she knew she'd die.

Standing by the door, she switched off the light. She immediately switched it back on. She wasn't scared of the dark, but she was scared of that lizard, and she wanted to be able to keep her eye on it at all times.

She got into bed and pulled the covers up to her chin for protection. Sounds from the street outside were filtering into the room. But she began to hear other sounds, too. Closer sounds. Sounds emanating from the wall behind her bed. She listened carefully, holding her breath. Either mice or giant cockroaches were holding the summer Olympics just inches from her head.

She froze, almost petrified. What if they all came in the room: the mice, the roaches—everything! She had to get out of there. Ariel didn't care if she had to spend the night walking the streets, she wasn't going to be locked up in a small room with numerous unfriendly species just waiting to launch an attack.

She got out of bed and put her shoes on first for fear of stepping on a living creature. She quickly got into her dress, then snatched up her purse and left the room. On the way to the elevator she stopped at Scott's door and knocked.

He came to the door naked, and she very carefully kept her eyes on his face. Although the sight of him nude was a lot more reassuring than the sight of that lizard had been.

"What's up?"

"I'll meet you in the lobby in the morning."

"I thought you'd be asleep by now. Is something the matter?" He looked like he'd had no trouble getting to sleep.

"I can't sleep in that room."

"I know it's not the height of luxury—"

"It's not even livable. At least not for humans." She was still maintaining her averted eyes although the pull of gravity seemed to be at work.

"Come on in—tell me about it." She gave a sigh of relief as he turned around, and she saw him reaching to pull on his briefs.

She looked carefully around the room before stepping inside the door. She couldn't see anything moving or even lurking in the shadows, but she was sure that if her room was inhabited, they probably all were.

She told him briefly about the lizard, the water bug, and the noises in the wall. His mustache seemed to twitch at one point, but at least he didn't laugh at her fears.

"You've got to expect that down here." True, but not reassuring.

"Maybe, but I don't have to like it. There's no way I could get any sleep in there, Scott. I think I'll just walk around all night."

"In Tijuana?"

"Since that happens to be where we are—"

"There are things a lot more dangerous out on those streets than a few bugs."

"I wouldn't care if there were lions out on those streets," Ariel shot back. "It's bugs I'm frightened of."

He moved toward her and put his arms around her, much as she would to comfort Nicole or Jody. But it wasn't comforting she needed; she needed assurance that there weren't any bugs around. Even while her cheek was pressed against his upper arm her eyes were moving around, peering into dark corners.

"Relax, Ariel."

She tried. She leaned against him, liking the warmth of his body, even finding herself getting turned on a little. But she couldn't force herself to close her eyes. And she hadn't come to his room to end up in his arms. She pulled away from him.

"I'll get out of here, Scott, and let you get some sleep. My phobias shouldn't keep both of us awake."

"I'm not all that eager to sleep."

"You were sleeping when I got here."

"But then I didn't have an alternative." He moved toward her again, but this time she turned around in an

effort to avoid him. He put his arms around her from
the rear, his hands resting on her stomach and the sides
of his arms pushing her breasts close together. His
mouth moved against her short curls as he said,
"Come on, let's go to bed."

"Scott!"

"I'm not propositioning you, Ariel. I'm just suggesting we get into bed. There aren't even any chairs in the
room; do you plan on standing up all night?"

She hadn't thought that far ahead. The bed was
large—they wouldn't have to come into contact at all.
Or was she deluding herself? Did she want to get into
bed with Scott? Did she want more than just getting
into bed with him?

He let go of her abruptly and got into bed, moving to
the far side and patting the empty space next to him.
"Come on, take off your dress and climb in."

"I'm not taking my dress off."

"Then leave it on. But you're going to get home
looking as if you slept in it."

She conceded that there was no point in arriving
home looking guilty, when she had no intention of
having anything to feel guilty about. "Turn away and
don't look," she ordered him, wishing now she had
dressed differently. It would have been a lot easier if
she'd worn a T-shirt and jeans.

He made an elaborate production of turning around
in the bed and covering his eyes with his hands. She
quickly pulled the dress over her head, then got into
her side of the bed, pulling the sheet up to her chin and
still clutching the dress in one hand.

"Can I look now?"

"Would you mind laying my dress across the dresser?'' She would have done it herself, but the dresser was on his side of the room, and she would have felt very exposed walking back to the bed topless.

He did as she asked, carefully smoothing out the dress so it wouldn't get wrinkled, then got back in his side of the bed and looked over at her. ''Anything else?''

''Are you going to leave the light on?''

''I figured you'd feel better with it on.''

''I would.''

''Then we'll leave it on.''

Her body felt rigid and she was scarcely breathing. She had never been in bed with a man before when the intention hadn't been to make love eventually. It felt unnatural somehow, and she knew her body was already beginning to react to stimuli that her mind rejected. She felt a pull toward him that had nothing to do with the fact that this bed, like the one in her room, sank in the center.

Ariel sneaked a look at Scott and saw that he was reclining outside the sheet, his hands clasped behind his head. Tufts of blond hair beneath his arms caught the overhead light, and his strong, fit body looked extremely desirable. Her attraction to him physically was indisputable, and she wondered at her perversity in refusing to make love with this man. She'd certainly never said no to her husband, even when the attraction hadn't been this strong.

He turned to her as though he realized there was a struggle going on in her mind. ''If I were to reach out and touch you right now, what do you think would happen?''

She turned to look at him, clutching the sheet in front of her. ''What do you mean?''

"Would a lightning bolt come down and strike you dead?"

She managed a smile. "No. At least I don't think so."

"Would the *policía* march into the room and arrest us?"

"I hope not."

"But do you think it's likely?"

She shook her head.

"Would it brand you in some way? Make you an unfit mother?"

That was a little closer to the mark. "I'm not sure."

"Ariel, are you afraid of falling in love with me?" His voice was low, almost a caress.

"I'd be afraid if I thought it was a possibility."

"Do you think there is?"

"I don't know. There's always that possibility, I'm afraid."

"But isn't that what makes life interesting? Possibilities?"

She didn't think it was interesting at all. She'd feel like a complete fool if she fell in love with a younger man. At least this younger man.

"How do you feel about me, Ariel?"

"I have a lot of conflicting emotions."

"Yes, I can see that. Do you want to talk about it?"

"No."

"Come over here and let me kiss you."

"You promised!"

"I don't recall promising anything." He rolled over closer to her, still not touching her body. Fingers as light as feathers reached out and traced her brows, then brushed against one cheek. His face was just inches from her own, his eyes holding hers in an unbreakable lock. She could feel his warm breath on her face; she could almost count each eyelash.

He had a strong face; she thought she'd never tire of looking at it. Lines from the sun spread out from his eyes, lines she'd never noticed before. He had more lines than she did, but then she didn't get that much sun. If only he had a few more lines, maybe some gray in his hair. That might make a difference.

"Touch me, Ariel." Softly, so softly.

She felt half mesmerized. One of her hands was coming out from beneath the sheet, and she found her finger tracing his mustache, then his lip. His lips felt dry, and she felt her own tongue come out to moisten her lips. In the silence she could hear her own breathing. Her eyelids felt heavy. Maybe if she closed her eyes it would be as though she weren't participating.

His face moved closer and she thought he was going to kiss her, but he shifted and she felt his rough chin moving back and forth against her cheek. Gently again; teasing her senses.

Ariel dropped her hand so that it was between them, but now she felt the springy hair on his chest, and her fingers reached through the hair to press against the skin. She felt like lifting the sheet and enclosing them both beneath it, shutting out the world.

Scott moved his hand and once more his mouth was just centimeters from hers, tantalizing her so that she wanted desperately to close the distance. If she were to lift her face just the slightest bit, their mouths would meet. Involuntarily, her lips parted.

"Kiss me, Ariel."

Why did she have to do it? Why didn't he stop all

this nonsense and just kiss her? She wasn't fighting him; not anymore.

"I'm not going to take advantage of you. If you want it, you're going to have to make the first move."

She'd never made the first move with a man. She didn't even think she was capable of it. Did he really have that kind of self-control that if she didn't kiss him first, he'd just roll right over and go to sleep?

She hesitated, her heart pounding. It couldn't end now; not now. She was feeling far too much to stop at this point. The consequences didn't even seem to matter anymore. All that mattered was making love with him, following the dictates of her body.

When it finally happened, she didn't know whether she'd moved her head upward or he'd lowered his. All she knew was the sensation of his lips closing over hers and the flood of desire that surged through her body. His kiss was gentle, and she felt her own lips grow more demanding when his tongue began to tease. She'd forgotten how absolutely delightful it was to lay beneath a man while their mouths began their exploration. For his body had soon lowered onto hers, and now she could feel the weight of him all along the length of her own body beneath the sheet. A sheet she no longer wished to come between them.

Her arms moved around his neck as her tongue began to probe in his mouth, their tongues meeting, circling one another, then moving off to investigate some more. But she wasn't an inexperienced girl satisfied by one kiss. Her entire body was longing now for his touch, as old desires stirred and made themselves known to her. Her skin felt as if it were on fire beneath the sheet, the rough-textured muslin an irritant. She began to feel frustrated as the kiss went on and on. Was this all it was going to be? Just a kiss? Was she still required to make the first move?

As their lips still clung together, he propped himself up on one elbow and began to pull the sheet away from her. She lifted herself up so that the twisted material could be pulled out from under her. When she lay uncovered at last, he lifted his mouth from hers, and she closed her eyes as his own took in her naked body on the bed. Then, deciding she'd rather see his expression than imagine the worst, she looked at his face and searched for a look of disappointment in his eyes. There was none, and she felt herself visibly relax.

Scott leaned over her, and she felt the tickling sensation of his mustache against her heated skin as his mouth traced the contours of her collarbone and then moved down the length of one arm. He pressed the palm of her hand against his mouth as his tongue moved in soft circles, and her fingertips caressed his face. Then he put her fingers into his mouth and bit them gently before he sucked on them and then held them there for a brief moment.

When his hand moved back to trace the puckered skin around one nipple, she found she could no longer differentiate one sensation from another. Her entire body had its nerves exposed, and touching her in one place triggered all the others. He was the most erotic, most accomplished lover she had ever been with, and she didn't even want to think about where he had gotten his experience. It was enough he had it at the moment. Enough that he could make her feel that every moment she had spent in bed with a man before had only been leading up to this moment, when an ordinary human being was being turned into a mass of molten flesh.

As his hand moved across exposed skin, his tongue followed, cooling only briefly her torrid flesh. Almost imperceptibly at first her body was lifting and falling, lifting and falling, foreshadowing the rhythms of love-making that now were inevitable. Her hands were moving up and down his torso, wanting to feel each inch of him and luxuriating in the feel. He didn't have an ounce of excess fat, just hard, smooth surfaces that warmed even more at her touch.

For a moment Scott's head rested on the soft curve of her stomach, then moved farther down. Ariel spread her legs and felt the first flicker of his tongue, realizing that the cry that came at his touch was from her. Still unhurriedly, he parted her fevered thighs and probed her again with the same slow insistence he had used on her mouth. It was all she could do to keep from thrashing about on the bed. She was near delirium as he forced her shattered nerve endings to focus inwardly until there was just one hot point that was steadily building, expanding, carrying her upward until she thought she could go no further, and then carrying her further still until she was poised precariously on some unseen summit wishing for nothing more than to be toppled over the edge and into oblivion.

When he finally entered her, it was as inevitable as the next ragged breath that was torn from her body. There was nothing slow about his lovemaking now. He seemed to have worked himself into the same level of frenzy to which he had brought her and they moved together, fitting their rhythms to each other as perfectly as their bodies were fitted. She tried to exert some control, to hold off until he was ready, but the pitch of her excitement was too great and she ineluctably exploded just moments before him.

Their bodies were covered with sweat and sticking together when at last they pulled apart and faced each other on the bed. She wanted to tell him what a powerful experience it had been for her, but the words wouldn't come. She didn't think he needed to hear it, anyway; it had obviously been the same for both of them.

"How about a shower?" he said to her.

Ariel nodded and followed him out of the bed. She felt totally satiated and relaxed and knew she'd have no trouble sleeping. The hell with bugs and lizards. With Scott beside her they had lost their threat.

She wouldn't have thought she could become aroused again so soon, but all it took was a bar of soap and his skillful hands, and they couldn't even wait to dry themselves off first. He picked her up and carried her back to the bed soaking wet, and this time she took some of the initiative as once again they made slow, delicious love in the steamy room. It appeared that once he had opened the floodgates to her emotions, she couldn't seem to get enough of his lovemaking. She was mentally and physically exhausted, but no sooner would she begin to doze off when the touch of his body against hers would once again trigger a response and they would come together once again until, near dawn, they both dropped off into fitful sleep.

Ariel awoke to sunlight streaming in through the glass doors to the balcony. She looked at her watch and saw that they had overslept; she was about to awaken Scott when, suddenly, she had second thoughts. She might have looked good to him in the dimness of the room the night before, but in the morning, in full sunlight, she was bound to look her age. As a matter of fact, she probably looked a lot worse than her age with the little sleep she had got.

She went quietly into the bathroom to study her face in the one available mirror. She saw that she didn't look any worse for wear, except that her face was rather pink. At first she thought it was from Scott's rough face, but then she realized the redness extended halfway down her chest and that she must have got some sunburn at the beach. Which was wonderful. The burn gave her a rosy glow, which added to her look of well-being. She was relieved to see she didn't look any worse in the morning than she did at any other time.

She went back to the room and shook Scott by the shoulder. When he opened his eyes, she said, "We'd better get going—it's after nine."

He gave her a lazy grin as he reached out to draw her down to the bed. "What's the hurry? A half hour more won't matter."

She didn't even put up a protest as their lips and bodies joined and coalesced once more into a single, pulsating organism. She had always loved sex in the morning, and today was no exception. She began to think of what it would be like to wake up each morning beside Scott, to reach for him and feel his response as their bodies joined to meet the new day together. Then all thought ceased as she was once again carried to dizzying heights that took her breath away.

When he finally released her to sit on the side of the bed and light a cigarette, she looked at him with awe. No wonder Sutton liked younger men, she thought. It wasn't only their bodies that were good. He seemed to have the energy of a teenager; an energy, she found, that matched her own.

"Any regrets?" he asked her.

She thought about it a moment, then shook her head. "Not at all," she said, smiling happily.

"Not struck by a bolt of lightning?"

She laughed. "Not in retribution, anyway."

"Have you fallen in love with me yet?"

"No, thank God!"

"Well, don't sound so happy about it. I wouldn't have minded."

"And here I thought I was easing your mind."

"Are you wondering why you put up such a fuss now?"

She nodded. "I honestly hadn't thought it could be like this. I loved the sex, and I feel we can still be friends. I owe you a lot for teaching me that, Scott."

She got up and put on her panties. She was amazed to find she was no longer the least bit modest in front of Scott. He had made her feel good about her body; so good, in fact, she wished they had the time to spend another day in Tijuana to visit the topless beach again. This time she'd get a tan all over. She pulled her dress over her head, then ran a comb through her short hair and applied a little lip gloss. Her lips felt swollen from his kisses, but she didn't think it was noticeable.

He was putting his own clothes on. "You in a hurry to get out of here?"

"I really have to get home."

"We ought to come down here again sometime."

"Well, maybe when I need more frames."

"It's still just a business trip to you, isn't it?"

She looked at him in surprise. "Not entirely. But I don't plan on making a habit of this."

"So, the sexual revolution has made a convert. Is it just going to be one-nighters for you from now on? Now that you've got the hang of it?"

She looked at him in dismay. Why was he trying to ruin the happiness of the moment? "I don't even know if you'd want to see me again." She had honestly thought that Scott was looking for a new experience, this time with an older woman.

"Why wouldn't I want to see you again? It was fantastic!"

She felt a surge of relief at his words. She would have hated to think he'd tire of her after only one night. She'd have to give it some serious thought, but she found it wasn't over for herself quite yet. "Let's just play it by ear."

He seemed somewhat mollified. "Let's just hope you sell those frames quick."

She'd been thinking the exact same thing. Although how she could use not reaching customs in time as an excuse again, she didn't know.

Chapter Eight

When they got back to the gallery, they were met by a welcoming committee. Nicole had opened the shop, Jody was playing sentry at the door, and Jack, a slightly different-looking Jack from the one Ariel remembered, was lying in wait.

She introduced the two men as she took in Jack's new look: slightly longer hair that appeared to be styled, running shorts and a tank top, and for a man who had previously worn only a watch, he was sporting an abundance of Indian jewelry. If the sexual revolution had finally hit her, he'd been hit by the youth culture, and it took all her self-control not to laugh out loud at his appearance.

While Jack helped Scott unload the van and carry the frames into the shop, the girls looked her over, as though determining whether she was the same mother they had seen off the previous day. Jody seemed quickly satisfied and went off to meet her friends. Nicole wasn't satisfied with just appearances.

"What'd you do in Mexico all night?" she asked Ariel.

"Had dinner, went to a movie, walked around. What'd you do last night?"

"Dad took us to Shakey's for a pizza. His girl friend came along."

"The one who wears Norma Kamali?"

Nicole nodded, but she was clearly not interested in pursuing the subject of her father's newest girl friend. "Do you like Scott?"

"Sure I like him. We're friends."

"That's all? Just friends?"

"Finding a friend is no small thing, Nicole."

Suspicion still lurked in Nicole's inquisitive eyes. "You're not in love with him or anything, are you?"

"Not at all, Nicole."

"You sure?"

"Very sure."

"He seems really nice, Mom. I just wondered, that's all."

"I can understand that."

Pacified, Nicole went upstairs to change for the beach. With no more than a breezy goodbye, Scott left, and Ariel found herself alone with her ex-husband.

"You're looking good, Jack," she said, thinking she should make mention of his new look.

"Are you sure I don't look a little ridiculous?"

He did, but no more than most of the middle-aged men around in similar garb. "You look fine," she assured him.

"I'm going with this girl. . . ."

"So the girls tell me."

"It's not easy, let me tell you."

"What's not easy?"

"Going with someone that young. The other night a

waiter thought I was her father. She thought it was funny, but I wasn't laughing. Listen, Ariel, are you interested in this guy? Scott?"

"We're just friends."

"He seems like a good guy, it's just that..."

"I know. He's young."

"There doesn't seem to be that much age difference. Anyway, you always looked young for your age. I mean, nobody's going to take you for his mother, that's for sure."

She didn't even want to be taken for his older girl friend. "I don't look young for my age."

"Sure you do—you don't even have a gray hair on your head. I'm almost half gray already, and I'm only a couple of years older than you."

"I don't see any gray, Jack."

"That's because I put something on it."

"You're dying your hair?"

"No, not dye. I wouldn't do that. It's just this stuff that gradually takes the gray away."

"You'd look good with gray hair."

"Yeah, good and old! I'm getting these lines, too, from being out on the water all the time."

"I think you're worrying unnecessarily, Jack. A lot of women go for older men. As a matter of fact, you're a lot better-looking now than you were when you were young."

"You really mean that?"

"Absolutely." And he'd look even better if he weren't trying so hard to look younger.

"Well, anyway, I think it's great that you're starting to go out, Ariel."

"I'm not going out, that was simply a business trip."

"Well, if he asks you out, I think you should go. He seems like a good guy."

"Why are you so interested in whether I go out?"

He gave a sheepish smile. "I guess if you were going out I wouldn't feel guilty about going out myself."

"There's no reason for you to feel guilty, Jack. We're divorced."

When Jack left, Ariel got out her invoice and computed the retail prices of the frames. She was affixing individual price tags to them when Sutton came in the front door with take-out food from Taco Bell.

"I hear you were in Mexico all night with Scott."

Ariel belatedly remembered she was supposed to have had dinner with Sutton the night before. "I'm sorry—I forgot all about calling you."

"Totally understandable, and I found out from the girls. So, did you have a good time?"

"It was fun."

"You spent the night in Mexico with that outrageously handsome hunk and all you can say is that it was fun?"

"We saw a Fassbinder film—"

"I don't want to hear about Fassbinder films. What happened?"

"What makes you think something happened?"

"Listen, you're not talking to your daughters now, Ariel. Or your ex-husband. Maybe they didn't notice a difference in you, but I happen to know the signs."

"What signs?"

"The signs of a satisfied woman. Now give!"

"Well, if it hadn't been for this lizard—"

"Never mind lizards! I want to hear about Scott."

"The lizard's important. If it hadn't been for the lizard, nothing would've happened."

"Clever lizard!"

Ariel gave an expurgated version of the night's events to Sutton, thinking it only fair in return for all the stories that came her way from her friend. Anyway, she had to talk to someone, and Sutton was her safest bet.

"So you found true love in a tawdry little hotel in Tijuana. I love it!"

"I didn't say anything about love."

"Substitute romance for love."

Ariel chuckled. "It was romantic, all right."

"I told you about young men, didn't I?"

Ariel nodded. "And you were right."

"Damn right I was. So are you going to see him again?"

"I don't see why not. So far I feel good about it, no guilt feelings at all."

"And you were so worried you couldn't handle casual sex!"

"I didn't know it would be that good. Is it always like that?"

"Unfortunately, no. But you really like him, don't you?"

"I like him a lot."

"That makes the difference. Of course, there's a thin line between liking him and loving the sex and loving him and loving the sex."

"That's what I thought. But if I didn't fall in love with him last night, I think I'm past the danger. Which is a big relief, let me tell you."

"Love can be fun."

"Love can be distracting! Don't tell me about love, Sutton, I've been there. If I hadn't fallen in love with Jack, I wouldn't have married at such an early age."

"Now that you've taken the plunge, you have no excuse for not going out with me."

"I go out with you all the time."

"Yeah, to dinner or the movies. I'm talking about going *out*."

"I don't think I'm ready for singles' bars."

"Who's talking about singles' bars? I'm invited to a party Friday night, and you're coming."

"I'll think about it."

"Never mind thinking about it, you're coming."

Ariel found herself smiling. "Sure, why not? If I like Scott, I might very well like other men."

She half expected Scott to stop by during the afternoon, but by the time she closed the shop he still hadn't appeared. She put a couple of her new frames in the window along with a badly printed sign that announced the arrival of a shipment of frames from Mexico. She sold six just that afternoon. She also spent some time reframing a few of her florals, and she thought they looked vastly improved with the new frames.

That night Ariel stayed home and played one of Jody's war games with her. It was all about capturing castles and mountains and took a little strategic thinking, more thinking than she was capable of doing with the little amount of sleep she had had the night before. At ten she made them cocoa and they were both asleep soon afterward.

By Wednesday Scott still hadn't appeared, but the shop was busy all day and she didn't give him much thought. In fact, the events of Monday night were beginning to take on a dreamlike quality. She thought of him at odd moments, but it hadn't blossomed into the kind of obsession she had been afraid of contracting. It was just a good feeling, and she found herself in a relaxed and happy state of mind.

The first thing Rose said to her when she arrived at her painting class Wednesday night was, "I hear you spent the night in Mexico with my son."

Ariel stopped dead in her tracks. "Your son?"

"Sure, didn't he tell you?"

Ariel thought back to all the references Scott had made to Rose. Not one of them had sounded like a son talking about his mother.

"But his last name's Campbell."

Rose chuckled. "I paint under my maiden name."

"I had no idea," said Ariel in a daze. "In fact..."

"In fact he makes fun of my painting, is that what you were going to say? Don't worry—we argue about it all the time. Nonetheless, I'm proud of him—he's the best painter in the family."

"He took me down there to get frames for my gallery," said Ariel, not wanting Rose to get the wrong idea. Actually, it was the right idea she didn't want Rose to get. What would the woman think of an older woman having an affair with her son?

"Listen, you don't have to explain to me. You're both consenting adults."

But she was a little more of one than he was. She felt herself blushing guiltily. "He's a very nice young man.

He's teaching some workshops at my gallery, did he tell you?"

Rose ignored the latter statement. "He's not all that young, Ariel. I, for one, think it's time he settled down."

Oh, Lord—was his mother going to play matchmaker? "He seems to know a lot of nice young women."

"Scott would never be satisfied with a nice young woman. I should know, he's gone through enough of them. You wouldn't believe all the phone calls he got from tearful young women when he lived at home. As a matter of fact, I think you'd be perfect for him. I wish I'd thought of it myself."

"You can't mean that, Rose. I'm much too old for him."

"How old are you, Ariel? About thirty-five?"

"Thirty-eight." *Now see if she thinks I'm still perfect for him*, Ariel thought with near triumph.

"So what's four years? Anyway, he'll be thirty-five in September."

"I thought he was younger than that."

"Didn't he tell you his age?"

"I was afraid to ask." And what a stupid thing to say. Now his mother would be sure she was interested in her son.

"Well anyway, Ariel, I didn't mean to embarrass you. I just wanted you to know you had my blessing."

"We're really just friends."

"More's the pity," said Rose with a doubtful look. Ariel got the feeling Rose was far more astute than she was giving her credit for. It was a little embarrassing, though, to be friends with the mother of the man she had made love with. Now she had one more person to worry about. Not that Scott seemed to be in any hurry to see her again. Maybe it was all over, and she was the last to know.

She didn't seem to be able to keep her mind on her painting that night, with the result that her mission turned out to be less than a masterpiece and she didn't feel it was even good enough to take out on the art show. And copying Rose's painting wasn't giving her the same satisfaction, she found, as doing original work in Scott's class. She didn't want to take sides, but maybe he did know something that Rose didn't. All she knew was that creating her own painting had given her a much better feeling than going home with another carbon copy of Rose's picture.

Ariel was giving Jody a lesson in oils in the back of the shop when Scott finally appeared on Friday. She noticed something different about him immediately but couldn't put her finger on it. Jody was more observant.

"What happened to your mustache?" she asked him.

Scott fingered his bare upper lip. "I needed a change." He looked over at Ariel. "What do you think?"

He looked just as good without a mustache as he did with one except that he also looked considerably younger. "I liked the mustache," she said.

He turned to Jody. "How about you?"

"I think you look better now. Younger."

Thanks a lot, Jody, thought Ariel. *Now he'll probably never grow it back in. Maybe if I let my hair grow and wore pigtails, we'd look okay together.*

Scott was grinning, as though he knew exactly why she preferred him with the mustache. She turned away and continued with her instruction to Jody. The girl was picking up the use of oils quickly but was more interested in pattern and color than in painting a picture that resembled anything.

A customer came into the shop and when Ariel got back from waiting on her, Scott was demonstrating different techniques with the knife to Jody. "She's got talent, your kid," he told her.

"She's been drawing since she was old enough to hold a pencil."

"Mom says when I learn about oils I can sit in on one of your workshops."

Ariel looked at Scott. "Would that be all right?"

"I'd love it. Kids are a lot easier to teach; they don't come with built-in hang-ups."

"What about tomorrow?" Jody asked him.

Scott looked at Ariel. "Do we have room?"

"She can have my place."

"No, I don't want you quitting on me. I'll bring a folding easel she can use."

"I can't afford—"

"Forget the money. I don't charge friends."

Since Scott had taken over teaching Jody, Ariel began to assemble her custom framing order. She was finding that with standard Mexican frames in stock she could save a lot of people money by circumventing custom framing, and the customers seemed appreciative. And the profits were just as good, with a lot less work for her.

At six she had most of the framing done, and she saw that Scott was helping Jody to clean up. She hadn't seen Scott since Monday and wished she could see him alone, but Jody showed no signs of leaving. She'd come to the conclusion that four years' difference in age wasn't enough to get excited about, but she wished he hadn't shaved off the mustache. Without it he didn't look a day over thirty, and that made an eight-year age difference, which was a whole new ball game. And she was getting tired of suddenly being put in the position where she was constantly thinking about her age.

"What are you doing tonight?" Scott finally asked, and of course it had to be the one night she did have something planned. It was his own fault, though, for having waited until the last minute.

"I'm going to a party."

Jody seemed more interested in the news than Scott. "You didn't say anything about going to a party."

"I'm going with Sutton."

Jody gave her a look of disdain. "Oh. To meet men."

"It's just a party, Jody."

"Maybe, but Sutton goes to parties to meet men."

Ariel was avoiding looking at Scott. Why couldn't he have asked her out for Saturday night? Why didn't he now? Or did he just expect her to be free whenever he felt like seeing her? Not that she could blame him for that assumption; she didn't exactly have a scintillating social life.

"I'll see you in the morning, then," he said, heading for the door. "And good hunting!"

"Did you have to say that about meeting men?" she said to Jody after the front door closed.

"Why else would you be going to a party with Sutton?"

Ariel shrugged. "To meet people, have a good time."

"To meet men."

"Jody, there are other things in life besides men."

"Tell that to Sutton!"

Ariel hadn't realized Jody paid such close attention to her conversations with Sutton. She'd have to start watching what she said around the girl, particularly if she was going to come out with embarrassing remarks in front of other people.

"What am I doing tonight, Mom?"

"Nicole's taking you to the movies."

"I don't want to go with her and her boyfriend. They're always kissing during the movie."

"Her boyfriend's away for the weekend."

"Are you going to be late?"

"Jody, you're not my mother!"

"Well, you've got to get up early in the morning."

"I know that. And I won't be late."

She wondered now why she'd even agreed to go to the party. She'd be terrible at a party. She hadn't been a single at a party since college; would she even know how to act anymore? She wondered what Scott had had in mind. Had he wanted to take her out or just over to his apartment for some sex? She thought she'd prefer the latter; she didn't think she was ready to be seen in public with him yet.

Of course it was just an assumption on her part that he had an apartment, but Rose had mentioned he didn't live at home anymore. Maybe he had roommates. Well, if he had roommates and she had two daughters at home, she didn't see any possibility of them ever getting together other than on some future trip to Tijuana.

And then she realized she hadn't even brought up the fact that she now knew Rose was his mother. Well, she'd mention it tomorrow. At least she'd be seeing him tomorrow.

She was dressed totally wrong for the party.

Ariel had dressed the way she used to dress for the parties she and Jack had gone to, but it was obvious from the moment she entered the house that these kind of Seal Beach parties didn't fit into the suburban mold. And it wasn't any consolation that Sutton was also dressed wrong, because Sutton could carry it off.

Ariel stood in the corner of the living room, half hidden by a large potted kentia palm as she sipped her vodka collins. She had worn a floor-length cotton dress with a halter top that gave her the look of a party chaperone rather than a party participant. Every other woman there—if you could call them women; they all looked eighteen maximum—was wearing jeans and a T-shirt, and she didn't think there was a bra worn by anyone in the crowd. And going braless beneath a T-shirt was a hell of a lot different than going braless beneath a halter dress.

And the men all looked like clones. From the styled hair, the Izod shirts, and the designer jeans, to the gold chains around their necks, each looked like a forty-year-old trying desperately to look twenty, and in some rare cases succeeding. Not one of them had done more than glance in her direction. Oh, there were a couple of exceptions. There were two young men who looked their age, but they were both in their early twenties. And they were both hanging onto Sutton's every word out on the patio.

"Is this your first time?"

The voice seemed to be coming from the palm before she glanced down and saw a middle-aged man sitting yogi-like on the floor.

"My first time at what?"

"Here. At the Friday nighters."

"You mean there's a party here every Friday night?"

"Sure. To meet people, you know?"

Good Lord, it was probably some kind of singles' club and Sutton had neglected to mention that fact. "Yes, it's my first time." And my last, she added to herself.

"You gotta relax. Let it all hang out."

"I'm relaxed."

"You don't look it. You look tense. Hey, you want a massage?"

"No, thanks."

"How about a joint? You wanna share a joint?"

"I'm fine. Really."

"Listen, don't let the competition get to you. Youth isn't everything. A lot of guys like older women."

What a lot of nerve he had. He was at least five years older than she was. "I really haven't entered the competition."

"Just checking it out, huh?"

She nodded. She was thinking of joining Sutton out on the patio when the man stood up and peered thoughtfully at her.

"You don't look too bad, you know. If you got an eye job you could pass for thirty. Easy."

At least she didn't have bags under her eyes the way he did. And no one had ever told her before that she needed an eye job. The nerve of the man! "I'm not interested in passing for thirty," she told him, wishing he'd get lost and leave her alone.

"How old are you, huh? Let me guess."

"Thirty-five." She instantly felt a sinking sensation in her stomach. It was the first time she'd ever lied about her age, and she couldn't believe she'd done it. And why? To impress this jerk standing next to her? She was about to amend it upward but didn't get a chance.

"Hey, that's not so old. You got a few good years left, you know what I mean?"

"Thanks." Her sarcasm was lost on him.

"It's okay. I know how it is. Hey, you want to feel my hair?"

She stared at him, sure she had heard him wrong.

"My hair. Run your fingers through it."

"No, thank you."

"Really. Be my guest." He grabbed her free hand and the next thing she knew it was being shoved through his oily black hair. "Just like the real thing, am I right?"

"The real thing?"

"Yeah. Hair transplants, you get it?"

"I never would have known."

"Cost me a bundle, but it was worth it. Girls like to run their hands through your hair, you know what I mean?"

She did know what he meant, unfortunately. But there was something about knowing it was a transplant that made her feel queasy. Transplanted from *where*?

"Hey, look at my eyes!"

His face was now so close to hers she was nearly looking cross-eyed at him. "Are they transplants, too?"

He laughed. "Hey, you got a sense of humor. I like that. No, they're contacts. Guess what color my eyes really are?"

At the moment they appeared to be an unlikely emerald green. "Blue?" she guessed.

"Right on the first guess! Green's a little more dynamic, you know what I mean?"

Ariel nodded, not even wanting to think about what he might show her next.

"Of course you girls can do a lot more with yourselves. I mean, we can't do silicone or anything like that." His eyes moved downward. "You ever thought of silicone injections?"

"Never."

"Yeah, well, it's not just for size, you know. Forget I said that; you probably don't need it yet."

Ariel glanced around for some means of escape, but there was no escaping Mr. Transplant.

"Fortunately, I've got a lot of body hair."

That was something she definitely didn't want to see.

"Otherwise I wouldn't have been able to get the transplants, you know what I mean?"

Ariel nodded.

"A lot of women like body hair, get turned on by it. A few don't, of course, but you can't win 'em all, I always say. What about you?"

"Me?"

"Yeah. You go for body hair?"

"I never thought about it."

"Of course I'm talking about men now, you understand. I don't like the way some women don't shave anymore. It's just not feminine, you know what I mean?"

"I never shave," Ariel informed him. Which was half lie and half truth. She shaved in the summer and didn't shave in the winter.

"Well, let me give you a little advice, and I hope you don't take it wrong. Not shaving isn't cute at your age, you know what I mean? I mean, some of these young girls might get away with it, but you need all the help you can get."

She looked at him in astonishment. Not only was he gross, he was highly insulting. She'd taken just about enough of his one-sided insults. "Oh, I don't know," she told him blithely. "The young men seem to go for it."

"Young men?"

"They seem to like me the way I am."

"You like young men?"

"Doesn't everyone?"

"I never figured you for—"

"The way I see it, over thirty is over the hill, if you get what I mean." She gave him a sympathetic smile.

"Hey, that's a fallacy. That's not really true, you know."

"Oh, it's true, all right."

"What's the matter with older men?"

"They tire so easily."

"Hey, not all of us."

"All of you," she said, staring him down.

"If you'll excuse me," he muttered, scurryng off to the bar.

She felt a momentary twinge. Not that he hadn't deserved it, but she really didn't like insulting people. She tried to imagine what he'd look like with a balding pate and horn-rimmed glasses. She wanted to believe he'd look better natural, but she couldn't be sure that was the case. Anyway, it was his obnoxious character that was in need of improvement, not his looks.

She was obviously not cut out for the singles scene, and she found herself feeling sorry for Jack, who was so obviously a part of it. No wonder his appearance was changing, if he had to contend with parties like this. She couldn't even remember what had prompted her to come. She was much happier staying home with the girls than going through this. And for what? A hop in the sack with some aging Lothario? No, thank you! And for that matter, there wasn't a man at the party who didn't make Scott look good in comparison. Even without comparison!

She glanced over at the bar and saw that Mr. Transplant had got his drink and moved on. Well, if she couldn't have a good time, at least she could get smashed. And a hangover tomorrow might serve to remind her never to come again.

She left her safe spot behind the kentia palm and walked over to the bar. She ordered a vodka martini this time, deciding to be daring, then drank half of it before heading for the patio where Sutton was now dancing with one of the young men. At least the music was good, sixties music she had danced to as a kid.

The young man Sutton wasn't dancing with beckoned her over. "You want to dance?" he asked her.

"I want to finish my drink first."

"Yeah, you need fortification for these parties."

"If you believe that, why did you come?"

"Jeff wanted to see Sutton again. I'm Alan."

"Ariel."

"Yeah? Pretty name."

"Thanks."

"You're Sutton's friend, right?"

She nodded. "We have shops across the street from each other."

"Your own business? That's great. I admire women who do things with their lives."

"I admire men who do things with their lives. What do you do?"

"Me? I'm still in college."

Ariel downed her drink and motioned to him that she was ready to dance. She didn't think she'd have much to talk about with a college boy, but at least they could dance. Why was she here, being insulted by a man and ending up dancing with a boy? Why didn't she just walk out, walk home, and chalk the evening up as a dead loss? She didn't even know what she'd expected. A party full of Scotts, all eager to be with her? He was probably a rarity, and if that was the case, maybe she shouldn't be so hard on him. All he'd ever done was to express a nice healthy interest in her, an interest she'd done her best to sabotage from the start.

The music ended, and Ariel walked over to Sutton. "I've got to get out of here."

"Not enjoying the party?"

"Try 'hating the party.'"

"I saw you talking to Herbie. Did you get to feel his hair?"

"You know him?"

"Everyone knows Herbie. He's harmless."

"I thought he was obnoxious."

"That too. I feel sorry for him, though. His wife left him, and he's trying so hard to recapture his youth."

"That's his problem, not mine." There was no way

Sutton was going to make her feel guilty for being rude to Herbie.

"Yeah, well, we all have problems."

"My only problem at the moment is this party. Would you mind if I left?"

"I'll get Alan to drive you home."

"Sutton, it's only six blocks. I'll walk."

"I'm sorry, Ariel. I thought you might get a kick out of the party. Maybe you should've stuck with Scott."

"Maybe you're right."

"Four years is nothing!"

"I don't know about that. Herbie suggested that I get an eye job."

Sutton burst out laughing. "Herbie's wife got an eye job right before she left him. I think she also got her rear end lifted."

Ariel was shaking her head in dismay. "That's what worries me about Scott. I don't think I can take a constant reminder of my age. I never even worried about it before, and now I'm becoming obsessed with how old I look."

"You don't look old."

"Yeah, but how do I know I won't fall apart before I'm forty? I never even gave it a thought with Jack, and I just hate it!"

"Scott doesn't seem worried about your age."

"Why should *he* worry? We're talking about my age, not his."

"Not everybody's hung up on age."

"Just everybody in Southern California!"

"It's not as if you're planning on marrying him, Ariel. Just enjoy yourself now, and worry about aging when it happens."

Ariel said goodbye to Sutton and noticed with amusement that no one else at the party even cared that she was leaving. It was past midnight, but the streets were still filled with people walking around on the warm summer night. Mostly in couples, but then, it was Friday night and only to be expected.

Once home she began a minute inspection of her eyes in the well-lighted mirror above the bathroom sink. She noticed a few lines, but didn't everyone who smiled have lines? She didn't think she saw the kind of creases and folds that signaled a need for an eye lift, but she knew that now she'd be constantly on the lookout.

She found herself thinking that despite the glorious weather, Southern California might not be the ideal place in which to grow old. Damn the youth culture for making her feel that way!

Chapter Nine

When the alarm clock went off the next morning, Ariel had an unaccountable urge to go right back to sleep. She was slightly hung over and mostly irritable, and she was feeling at least a hundred years old. Maybe two.

How long had it been since she'd had a day off? She couldn't even remember. Sundays certainly didn't count, as she was up at dawn and out at the art show until the sun went down.

The hell with everything, she decided, rolling back over onto her stomach and pulling the sheet up over her head. Would the world come to an end if she didn't get up? She doubted it. Would commerce as we know it grind to a halt? Not likely. Would nine irate students summon the police and/or break down the door to her gallery? Yes, indeed, that was a possibility.

She sat up with a groan.

"What's the matter, Mom?" Nicole's voice floated in from the kitchen.

"Just once. Just once in my whole entire life, I'd like to be able to sleep until noon. But, Nicole, since there isn't any justice in this world..."

Nicole came into the room and handed her a mug of

coffee. Well, there was some justice in the world, she decided. At least for the first time in her life she was being served coffee in bed. And if she'd had a little foresight years ago, this could have been a daily occurrence.

"Thank you, Nicole, you're a sweetie."

Nicole sat down on the edge of the bed, and Ariel found herself studying her daughter's eyes. No, no lines—not even a circle under them. But then, she was just a child. Nobody had lines at fifteen.

"You can sleep until noon if you want, Mom."

"I wish that were so, but it isn't."

"Why not? I'm opening the shop."

"There's the class."

"I'll set up the easels for you, and Scott should be able to handle the rest."

"Oh, Nicole—if I thought for a moment..."

"I mean it, Mom. Jody's taking the class today, isn't she?"

Ariel nodded.

"Well, she can help Scott. Go on, Mom—sleep till noon if you want. Then you could go to the beach and get a suntan. It's not fair; Dad gets weekends off, but you're always working."

Truer words were never spoken.

"Anyway, you look like you could use some more sleep. Your eyes are all puffy and—"

"Not the eyes, Nicole; don't mention the eyes!"

"They're even bloodshot. Were you drinking last night?"

Could a few shots of vodka be considered drinking? Obviously so, if her eyes were bloodshot as a result. "I had a little to drink."

"How was the party? Meet any men?"

"There was one real sweetheart named Herbie...."

Nicole giggled. "I'll bet, with that name."

Ariel finished the coffee and sank back on the pillow. "You really think you could handle everything without me?"

"Well, if there was an emergency, you're right up-stairs."

"You really wouldn't mind?"

"I don't mind at all. You just go right back to sleep and I'll even fix Jody's breakfast. Go on now, I mean it!"

With a blissful smile directed at her daughter, Ariel closed her eyes.

The next time she woke up, the clock said eleven-thirty. Not quite sleeping until noon, but almost as good. And what was more, she felt a hundred percent better. She studied her eyes long and hard in the mirror. A little bloodshot, but nothing Visine wouldn't cure. No bags. No pouches. A few lines, but only if she looked closely. Maybe she should start wearing sun-glasses.

Ariel made herself another cup of coffee, then hunted around in the closet for her bathing suit. It was one piece and black, and she couldn't imagine why she'd ever bought it. She was so used to seeing Nicole and her friends in their bikinis that her suit looked like an anachronism. Well, was there any law saying she couldn't buy a new one? Particularly since it was August, and they were all on sale? No, there was not. She would shop for a new one and wear it to the beach from the store. And maybe she would get some sunglasses.

She put on her old suit and wore a shirt on top of it

that came to her knees. She borrowed a pair of Nicole's rubber thongs to wear on her feet, then grabbed one of the girls' beach towels and stuffed it in her straw bag along with a book to read. She might even treat herself to brunch on the way to the beach.

She entered the shop by the back door and tried to go through the room quietly and not disturb the students. She was spotted by Jody, however, and waved over to see her picture.

Ariel didn't know whether to laugh at the effort or applaud it. It was very well done from the sky right down to the almost deserted beach. It was the object behind the one lone rock that nearly made her laugh. A man, dressed in camouflage, was pointing a rifle at an unseen enemy. Of course, it probably wasn't a man. It was, no doubt, a self-portrait.

"She's amazing, isn't she?" Scott's voice was heard behind her.

Ariel nodded. "I'm very impressed."

"Defecting from my class, Ariel?"

Ariel turned around to face him. "I felt desperately in need of a day off, and my daughters granted my wish."

His eyes were mocking. "Didn't you consider last Monday a day off?"

"I forgot about that."

He raised one brow in disbelief.

"I just mean that I considered that business."

His other brow joined the first.

Ariel moved out of earshot of Jody. "You know very well what I mean," she hissed at him.

He gave a low chuckle. "So how was the party last night?"

"Dreadful."

"Glad to hear it."

"And speaking of being dreadful, why didn't you tell me Rose Saunders was your mother?"

"Are you calling my mother dreadful or have you at last come to the realization that her pictures—"

"I'm calling you dreadful for not telling me!"

"I figured you'd hear about it sooner or later."

"Did you have to tell her we spent the night in Mexico together?"

He grinned. "I have no secrets from my mother."

"I hope you don't mean that, Scott."

He laughed. "She happens to think we're a perfect couple."

"So I was informed."

"I happen to think so too."

"Perfect for what?" Ariel muttered, trying to get past him.

He grabbed hold of her arm and bent down to whisper in her ear. "I think you know what we're perfect for, Ariel."

Ariel could feel herself blushing as she pulled her arm loose and went into the front of the shop. She was afraid he'd follow her and say something in front of Nicole, but blessedly, he desisted.

"You going to the beach now, Mom?"

"I thought I would, unless you need me."

"Everything's fine—you just have a good time."

Once out of the shop, she felt as if she were playing hooky from school. She walked slowly down Main Street, pausing to look into shop windows, while hoards of beachgoers circled around her. When not looking in shop windows, she found herself studying the women on the street. Their eyes in particular caught her attention, those women who weren't wearing sunglasses. She tried to assess their ages, and for the most part she felt she failed. It seemed to her that there wasn't a gray head or an unfit body in the crowd, not even among the women who, she felt sure, were as old or older than she was.

An obsession—no doubt about it!

The bikinis in the window of a boutique called The Beachcomber caught her eye, and she went inside to look around. The saleswomen all looked about fifteen years old, and they were all wearing short shorts and bikini tops. Ariel almost turned around and walked back out, but the thought of her hideous black bathing suit stopped her.

She found three she thought were possibilities—a pink concoction made of T-shirt material, a beige knit, and a Hawaiian print. She was allowed into the communal dressing room with them only after checking her large straw bag, and once inside she was informed by yet another pubescent female that she'd have to try the suits on over her own, as trying on bathing suits without wearing underwear beneath was against the law.

She pulled down the top of her suit with a sudden, new feeling of modesty. She couldn't remember enduring communal dressing since the shower room in her college dorm. She was hoping no one would notice her. A quick glance around told her that the young girls also trying on suits were too engrossed in looking at their own budding bodies to pay any attention to hers.

The beige suit wouldn't do at all. The top so nearly blended in with her body that she knew she'd look nude from a distance wearing it. Between the pink and the Hawaiian print, she preferred the pink, and having decided to buy it, she persuaded the overseer of the dressing room to allow her to wear it out, once having had the tags cut off, of course.

Feeling cavalier and daring, she left the shop with her shirt unbuttoned and her new bikini showing beneath. Daring for her: Everyone else going to the beach wore bathing suits with nothing over them.

A sidewalk café on Ocean Avenue was still serving breakfast, and she took a seat at one of the tables, ordering a mushroom omelet, orange juice, and coffee. All around her young people in couples and groups were enjoying the glorious day, and no one gave her a second glance—in most cases not even a first. She felt invisible, effectively cut off from view by nothing more than her age.

Ariel was allowing one young man to imbue her with paranoia. Whereas before she hadn't given a thought to birthdays, had in fact bragged about being middle-aged while not believing it for a minute, now . . . Now? Now she was fast becoming a basket case. Why Scott? Why couldn't some distinguished older man have become attracted to her, a man who would make her feel young and whom she could sympathetically console on his own signs of aging? And most of all, why did the attraction have to be mutual? Why couldn't she have ignored him, laughed it off for the silly thing it was? She hated being put in the position of being the experienced "older woman." Hell, she wasn't even that experienced!

Scott was simply amusing himself with her and, in doing so, was opening her up for ridicule. Why in the world was he even wasting his time? At thirty-four he should be looking for a future partner, some young woman he could settle down with, with whom he could start a family. So he thought marriage was the kiss of death to an artist, so what? He'd change his mind when the right woman came along, sooner or later, when he fell in love. And by no stretch of the imagination was she that woman. She'd been through all that, the diapers, the nightly feedings. In a few short years, she'd probably be a grandmother. She didn't regret those years, but there was no way she was going to go through them again.

She wondered if Jack would end up marrying one of his young girl friends and start a second family. A lot of men did and very successfully, but she couldn't quite see Jack in that role. He'd been irritable enough when their own two were babies, when his nightly sleep was constantly interrupted. And he'd been young then.

And why was she taking the whole thing so seriously, anyway? She should just enjoy Scott for the moment, look upon him as a summer romance that she'd look back on in the winter as an amusing interlude in her mundane life. She was working herself into a fervor over something she would have taken in stride at twenty. Forget her age! Forget the age difference! What would it all matter a year from now?

Her omelet arrived looking more like scrambled eggs than an omelet. It did, however, have the attraction of having not been cooked by herself, and she never went to the trouble of cooking with mushrooms on her own. As she ate she watched the people passing on the sidewalk. A group of young girls would pass, and every male head would lift and turn to follow their progress. Anyone over thirty seemed cloaked in the same invisibility as she was. She wondered what the reaction would be if Jane Fonda passed by in a bikini. The actress was several years older than Ariel, but didn't she still get roles that featured her as a desirable woman? In fact, wasn't she married to a younger man? Would they even notice her if she walked by?

Probably not. To watch her on a movie screen was one thing; to have her walk by in the flesh was surely another.

She paid her check and then walked to the corner drugstore, purchasing suntan lotion and a pair of over-sized sunglasses with translucent red frames. By the time she walked down the steps to the beach it was almost wall-to-wall bodies, and she found a spot between a group of teenage boys and two young mothers with children.

She spread out her towel, removed her shirt and applied the lotion to the ninety-nine percent of her body that was not covered by the miniscule bikini. She noticed that when she moved, the small top—perched precariously on her breasts—did not necessarily move with her. She hoped it would survive a swim in the ocean.

Ten minutes of lying on her back reminded her of the reason she wasn't tan. Lying on the beach doing absolutely nothing was boring. It had been different in school, when there'd been groups of friends and frequent swims and volleyball games. Now it was simply enforced idleness, and she could suddenly think of a million things she'd be better off doing. Nonetheless, she did need some color, and if this was the only way to get it . . .

She waited another ten minutes, then rolled over on

her stomach, making sure her top rolled with her. Maybe an hour of this would be enough. Any more and she might risk getting burned, mightn't she? All that this laziness was doing for her was giving her the time to think about things best left not thought about. She would have accomplished more in the painting workshop. Which reminded her of Scott. Which reminded her of her age. And if she didn't get over this phobia of hers quickly, she was going to scream!

In frustration, she got up and headed for the water. She walked in up to her chest, then plunged beneath a wave and swam out beyond where the breakers were forming. Bodysurfing back in, she concentrated on her top not falling off, but on her way back to her towel she looked down at herself and noticed something as bad. Her little unlined suit was now effectively transparent and clinging to cold, erect nipples. And the bottom was worse! For once she was thankful no one paid any attention to her.

One hour more of sunbathing and she'd had it for the day. She put on her shirt, packed up her bag, and headed for Sutton's shop. Sutton was in the back doing alterations, and Ariel helped herself to a cup of coffee before she sat down.

"You doing anything tonight, Sutton?"

"Not a thing."

"I was thinking of driving down to the art festival in Laguna. Want to come along?"

"A lot of men down there?"

Ariel gave her an exasperated look. "Is that all you think about?"

"What else is there?"

"Culture."

"You can take the culture. I'll take the men."

"Anyway, I've got to take Jody along."

"Well, then, since you have company for the outing, I think I'll pass."

"Sutton, I think I'm in need of a shrink."

"What's the problem?"

"I'm becoming obsessed with my age."

"Don't worry about it, Ariel. That's called the Southern California Syndrome, and we're all afflicted with it sooner or later. I got my first symptoms when I reached forty."

"It's disquieting. I never gave my age a thought before."

"You didn't have a young lover before."

Ariel watched Sutton light a cigarette and thought that, on occasion, it would be nice to smoke. Calmed the nerves, didn't it? But she'd also heard it caused lines around the mouth, and—there she went again, worrying about signs of aging! "Why can't I handle a simple four-year age difference?"

"Does Scott ever mention it?"

"Never. He never even told me how old he was; I had to find that out from his mother."

"Does he know how old you are?"

"I told him, but he could have figured it out easily enough by Nicole's age. I don't think he cares."

"I don't know what to tell you, Ariel. This is obviously your obsession, not his. Would it do any good to tell you that at times you don't look a day over thirty?"

"What about the other times?"

Sutton shrugged. "You look your age. But thirty-eight isn't old." She reached for *Elle*, the French fashion magazine, and handed it to Ariel. "Look on page 112."

Ariel flipped through the magazine until she came to an interview, complete with pictures, of Brigitte Bardot. The actress was a good ten years older than Ariel, yet here she was, in one photograph nude, looking even better than she had at twenty.

"Is this supposed to make me feel better?"

Sutton laughed. "It made me feel better. And her boyfriend's quite a bit younger, you know."

"She's probably had plastic surgery."

"Over every inch of her?" asked Sutton in an incredulous tone. "I'm just trying to point out to you that you have quite a few good years left. Look at all the women in their fifties who still look great."

"They probably spend a lot of time on it."

"So put some skin cream on your face at night."

Ariel grimaced.

"You're impossible, you know it? I'll bet if you didn't have those two kids you'd be saying you were thirty, and everyone would believe you. I don't think it's your age that's bothering you, anyway. Nor the age difference. I think you're afraid of falling in love with Scott, and you're just using the age as an excuse to talk yourself out of it."

"Baloney," said Ariel, after discarding the first word that came to mind.

"I think you're afraid that if you get too close to him he'll leave you the way Jack did."

"I think you're trying to psychoanalyze me, Sutton."

"I know you weren't broken up about the divorce, but didn't it do something to your ego when Jack started dating all those young women?"

Ariel tried to give it some serious thought. "I don't think so, Sutton. I just think he's kind of pathetic."

"Maybe to you he is, but other men his age probably regard him as a real swinger."

"Jack needs someone younger; I was always too strong for him. He would have done much better with a docile young wife who looked up to him and thought he was marvelous."

"There are a lot of men like that. There's also a lot of men who like strong, intelligent women, and Scott's probably one of them. Does he seem young to you when you're with him?"

Ariel shook her head. On the contrary, he had seemed more experienced and knowledgeable in the two areas they had pursued the most, art and sex.

"You wearing a bathing suit under that shirt?"

"Uh—I just bought it. My old one made me look like Mother Hubbard."

"Take off the shirt and let me see."

"Sutton—"

"I mean it, let me get a look at you."

Ariel reluctantly stood up and removed her shirt, making sure to pull in her stomach. Brigitte Bardot she was not!

"Turn around, let me get a good look."

Ariel complied.

"You don't even sag! Not anywhere."

"I have stretch marks."

"Where?"

Ariel looked down and finally located a couple on the inside of her thighs, pointing them out to Sutton as though she'd made a great discovery.

"Big deal! You can hardly find them."

Embarrassed, Ariel put her shirt back on and sat

down. "I know I look okay now. But what about when I'm fifty and he's only forty-six?"

"You're already projecting the future?"

"I've given it a little thought."

"He could be bald by then. Or gray. Why can't you just enjoy him and not worry about twelve years from now? I never knew you were such a worrier, Ariel."

"Usually I'm not." She picked up her bag and stood up. She ought to get back to the shop before the class ended, in case she was needed for anything.

"Listen, Ariel. Just stop worrying about anything. You look great; any man would be proud to be seen with you. Just try to have a better image of yourself, okay?"

"I'll try."

"And don't overdo the sun. It causes lines, you know."

Just what she needed to hear!

Back at the shop Scott had already left, and Nicole was helping Jody clean up the back room.

"How did it go?" she asked them.

They both spoke at once, Nicole telling her of the business she had done and Jody speaking almost worshipfully about Scott's class. She left them to finish the cleaning and went upstairs to shower. She'd take them both to the Green Pepper for a Mexican dinner before she and Jody headed down to Laguna.

Ariel glanced into the rear view mirror and chuckled. "Lower that rifle, Jody. Someone's going to think it's real and go off the road."

Jody did as she was told, but pulled the pin from her

phony hand grenade and lobbed it into the front seat
beside her mother, causing Ariel to wonder when the
child was going to get over her obsession with guerrilla
warfare. The previous summer Jody had been a completely normal child, albeit still a tomboy.

The traffic was heavy on Pacific Coast Highway going down to Laguna Beach, but Ariel enjoyed the ride
along the coastline. What she didn't enjoy was the
bumper-to-bumper traffic when she reached Laguna,
with everyone trying to find a parking spot for the festival.

She finally found a parking place a couple of miles
from the festival grounds and could only hope the tram
came down that far.

"Why don't you leave your rifle and helmet in the
car?" she suggested.

Jody left the rifle, but the helmet stayed on her head,
adding the final touch to her combat fatigues. It was
more of a concession than Ariel had expected, so she
didn't say anything more.

They only had to walk a couple of blocks up the highway to catch the tram, and Jody seemed to enjoy the
ride in the open cars. People came from as far as Los
Angeles and San Diego to see the yearly art festival,
and Ariel was beginning to think Saturday night hadn't
been a good choice. During the week it would undoubtedly have been less crowded.

Many well-known and important artists lived in and
around the Laguna Beach area, and most of them par-
ticipated in the art show. It was by invitation only, and a
panel of experts decided who qualified and who did
not. Ariel thought that perhaps in a few years she might
have accumulated a body of work she could submit

herself, but it couldn't be the kind of work she did in Rose's class. The commercial types of artists who went out on the art shows in the malls were never allowed into the festival.

She bought tickets for them both at the admission booth, and then they started down the first aisle of exhibits. The sales booth would take care of purchases if the artists weren't there, but most of them were sitting in front of their exhibits, answering questions for interested patrons.

In addition to paintings and lithographs, there were also displays of sculpture and handcrafted jewelry, but she wasn't as interested in these. Now if Nicole had been along the jewelry booths would have been the main attraction, but Jody's tastes nearly paralleled her own. The predominant theme of the Laguna Beach painters was the ocean in its various guises, but Ariel's personal favorite was Marco Feranzi, whose career she had been following for years. When she reached his display, she stood back to look at it as a smile spread over her face.

He always surprised her, each year coming up with something totally different. Not the style, which remained distinct, but the subject matter. This year, instead of painting the beauty of Southern California as most of the artists did, his enormous canvases depicted such mundane subjects as the inside of a gigantic medicine cabinet, an old refrigerator with the door hanging open, and a used-car lot. He could take the most innocuous subjects and make them a joy to behold.

The artist himself was sitting in front of his display. She had seen him before, but in other years she hadn't been in the habit of assessing men. Now she found that she was. Good-looking without a doubt with his dark, curly hair, matching beard, and a gold hoop in one ear adding to his particular brand of piratical charm, she saw that he was also appraising her, and from his reaction he liked what he saw.

"You like what you see?" he asked her, and she had a feeling he was talking about himself rather than his work.

She was feeling pretty good about herself, with her newly acquired tan setting off the white cotton jumpsuit she was wearing. "Very much," she replied, leaving the answer ambiguous.

"What in particular catches your discerning eye?"

She was tempted to tell him it was his earring, but instead turned to the painting of the medicine cabinet. "You always manage to do the unexpected. It never would have occurred to me to paint a medicine cabinet, but it's marvelous."

Like all artists Marco seemed to thrive on praise. His smile widened, making the corners of his dark eyes crinkle up in a becoming way. Ariel found herself wondering how old he was.

"Can I take that to mean you also paint?"

Ariel caught Jody watching this exchange with suspicion and felt herself flush. Was she flirting with this man? She not only decided that she was, she also decided she was enjoying it.

"I try," she admitted.

His eyes were on her jumpsuit, where they paused momentarily at her waist where a double belt accentuated her curves. "What do you paint?"

She wasn't about to say florals, but she had a feeling that wasn't what he was interested in anyway. "At the moment I'm experimenting with fog."

"Well, if you ever feel like experimenting with medicine chests, I happen to have an interesting one only a few blocks from here."

Jody's suspicion was turning into something more concrete, and Ariel saw the girl move on to the next exhibit, but not before throwing her mother a glance that clearly said: Refuse to follow me at your own peril!

"I have a medicine chest at home too."

"Well, then, I'd be glad to experiment with yours."

Living in a part of the country filled with blond men, Ariel had always found dark men devastatingly attractive. What would it be like to paint with Marco Feranzi? Hell, was she kidding? What she was really wondering was what it'd be like to make love with Marco Feranzi.

"What's your name?"

"Ariel Ryan," she said, using her maiden name, which was also the name she put on her paintings.

"Not Red Ryan's daughter?"

Did everyone in the world know her father? She nodded.

"How's Red doing? I hear he's down in Mexico."

"All I get from him is an occasional postcard, but he seems to be doing fine."

"Does he still have that place in Seal Beach?"

"I have it now," she told him, realizing that now he not only knew her name but where he could find her. With that accomplished, she decided she'd better move on before Jody became lost in the crowds.

"I'll be seeing you, Ariel," she heard him say as she walked past him in search of Jody.

She was feeling very good about herself by the time she caught up with Jody. Obviously, artists had more

discernment than the average man on the street. If
Scott found her attractive, and obviously Marco did,
then what was she so worried about? She suddenly felt
young and desirable and wasn't even concerned by
Jody's obvious disapproval.

"You were flirting with that man," Jody grumbled.

"Why not? I admire him."

"You're too old to flirt."

"You're never too old to flirt," she corrected her
daughter, thinking it a very Sutton-like remark but enjoying it anyway.

Her enjoyment of the situation turned to astonishment as they turned the next corner and she practically
walked into Scott, who was sitting in front of his own
display.

"What are you doing here?" she asked in bewilder-
ment.

He gave her an easy grin. "Getting rich and fa-
mous."

Chapter Ten

"I thought you were a starving artist!"

Scott laughed. "Sorry to disappoint you."

Ariel turned in confusion to look at his display. Jody was already poring over his *Banana Republic* and turned to her mother with shining eyes.

"Aren't they great?"

"I knew you'd like them." Here she thought she'd been doing Scott a favor by allowing him to teach at her place, while all the time the positions had been reversed. No wonder so many people had flocked to the classes. Obviously they had heard of him, even if she hadn't. She noticed several sold signs beside his paintings and picked up one of his brochures, curious to see what he charged for them. The amount of the prices astounded her. Starving artist! Why, he must be rolling in money!

"I didn't see you here last year."

"I was out of the country," he reminded her.

And before that she'd always attended the festival with Jack, a very disinterested Jack, who had dragged her through the aisles so fast she never got a chance to really study anything. And yet she had remembered Marco....

"You're looking good," he told her. "You sure tan fast."

He was looking good himself. Unlike Marco, who'd been wearing cut-off jeans and a T-shirt, showing off his muscular body, Scott was dressed in a tan gabardine suit with a dark brown shirt beneath.

Feeling self-conscious under his scrutiny, she turned and began to study his paintings. Like the ones done in class, they were all large squares, rather impressionistic, and all simple landscapes with just one lone object in the foreground. Her favorite was of a deserted field that had hills in the background. An old carousel tilted precariously nearby; its wooden horses looked so real she felt she could reach out and touch them and feel the peeling paint. They all had a lonely, sad feel to them, unlike his humorous prints. The price on the piece was eight thousand dollars, but if she had the money she'd buy it and consider the money well spent. It was the kind of picture she could get lost in just looking at it.

"You like that one?" He had come up beside her, so close she could feel the electricity humming between them.

"I love it."

"You're a romantic at heart, Ariel."

"I'm no such thing!"

"You mean you'll admit to no such thing."

"I want to do drawings like these, Scott," Jody was saying.

"Then what's stopping you?"

"If I do some, will you look at them?"

He put his hand on the girl's shoulder. "Try and stop

me. You've got the talent, Jody. You can do your own guerrilla suite."

He'd made one convert among her daughters, Ariel noticed. Not that this meant Jody would like him for her mother, just that she liked him around for herself.

"What are you two doing later?" he asked her.

"Going, home."

"Why don't you come to a party, meet some of the artists? There'll be kids there," he added for Jody's benefit.

"Can we, Mom?"

"I have to get up early—"

"You don't need to stay late," Scott assured her. "Stop back here around eleven and we'll go together."

Now that Ariel had seen what was being done by the Laguna artists, she wasn't altogether sure she even wanted to go out on her art show anymore. Not that she'd quit; she needed the money too much for that. But she didn't think she'd be content to paint just florals anymore. She wanted to paint medicine cabinets, carousels...No, that wouldn't be any more original than her florals. What she wanted was the time to find her own style. But that kind of time right now was in very short supply.

"What're you thinking about, Ariel?"

"I was thinking about what you said to me the day we met. About time being an artist's most valuable commodity."

"You agree with me now?"

"I'm beginning to."

"I'm glad to hear I'm making progress with you. Stick with me and you'll be a changed person."

She gave him a dubious look. "Are you setting your-self up as my Svengali?"

He laughed. "Nothing so extreme." He bent closer to her so as not to be overheard by Jody. "You must know I like you just the way you are."

"Quit flirting with all the artists, Mother!"

"All the artists?" asked Scott.

"Jody equates talking with a man with flirting."

Jody gave her an enraged look and Ariel couldn't blame her. She had most definitely been flirting with Marco, and even an eleven-year-old could tell the dif-ference between flirting and ordinary conversation. She just wasn't finding it easy to say anything to men with kids around. It was rather like having built-in censors.

She finally agreed to go to the party with him for a little while. When reminded by Jody that she'd slept all morning, she couldn't find any excuse not to. She'd get to bed early the following night.

They continued browsing through the exhibits, then crossed the road from the festival grounds to where the Laguna Arts and Crafts Fair was being held simulta-neously. In contrast to the Art Festival, this was a place where any craftsman could rent a space for a fee. As a result, the work wasn't necessarily of the highest qual-ity, but it also wasn't nearly as expensive. While hippies were now a dying breed in California, the last remnants of them could be seen here, selling everything from copper jewelry to hand-painted rocks. There was also food to be had, and Ariel and Jody filled up on differ-ent ethnic delicacies as they wandered from stall to stall.

When they returned to the festival grounds Scott was waiting for them, and they all took the tram to where she had parked the car. Scott left his at the festival, telling her he could get a ride back there with one of the artists.

The party was held in a house up in the hills of Laguna, and they could see people milling around the front of the house as they approached. As Scott had promised, there were plenty of children present, and Jody, never shy in the company of her peers, was quickly assimilated into their midst, leaving Ariel to enter the house with Scott.

There were people of all ages, and Ariel recognized many of the artists from the show. She felt like a fan suddenly thrust into a gathering where all the artists she admired the most were together in one place, and she hoped that Scott would keep quiet about her own artistic endeavors. She felt like an impostor in the group and wondered why she had ever felt it was an accomplishment she'd been accepted on the Sunday art show. She was sure these people had never stood on street corners or inside shopping malls hawking their works. These were people whose careers had begun with gallery shows and who had now secured a position in the art world.

Still, it was a far cry from the singles' party she had attended just the night before. She didn't feel old or unattractive, nor did she feel any embarrassment to be seen here with Scott. He was pulling her through the crowd by the door, introducing her to someone new at each step, so quickly that she knew she'd never keep the names straight.

Lights were strung outside in a garden beyond French doors, where picnic tables held various varieties of food and drink. Scott had handed her a can of beer before he took one for himself when a deep voice behind her said, "You've come to me, and here I thought I'd have to come to you."

A hand on her shoulder told her the words had been meant for her, and Ariel turned to see the beginnings of a smile on Marco Feranzi's face.

"Do I have you to thank for this?" he was asking Scott. "If so, you're more of a buddy than I thought."

"She's with me, Marco."

"For the moment. Only for the moment."

Scott turned to Ariel with a laugh. "Ariel, this is—"

"The lady and I have already met."

Nonetheless his hand was reaching for hers, and Ariel soon found her hand enclosed in both of his large, warm ones. She was still trying to think of something to say when Marco saved her the trouble.

"I think it must be fate, two times in one short evening."

"Hardly fate, Marco," drawled Scott.

"Not fate? For you to deliver her to my doorstep?" Marco's voice conveyed that only a miracle could have been responsible.

"Do you believe in fate?" he murmured to Ariel.

"Not really," she answered, disconcerted by the knowledge that she was standing between two men and she felt a physical attraction for both.

If he was disappointed in her answer, he didn't show it. "Come along, I will show you my studio," he said to her.

Ariel looked at Scott for rescue, but his expression of amusement told her she was on her own. Well, if he didn't care, she didn't; and she would like to see Marco's studio. She was always interested in seeing other artists' studios.

Marco led her down four stone steps to where a separate building built mostly of glass was nestled between a small grove of olive trees. He ushered her inside, then flicked a switch by the door that flooded the room with light.

She was just beginning to look around when he unceremoniously took the can of beer from her hand and said, "I have something more suitable to the occasion." He went to a small refrigerator and removed a bottle of champagne, then led her over to a small couch where he tried to seat her, but she evaded his tactics and took a seat in a chair instead.

"What makes champagne more suitable than beer?" she inquired.

Marco poured them each a glass and handed her one. "Do you want to hear prevarication or do you prefer the truth."

"The truth."

"I figure it will loosen you up faster."

"Loosen me up for the kill?"

"Ah, I see I don't have to play games with you. You believe in coming straight to the point, do you?"

"I prefer honesty."

He lifted one scraggly brow. "Between women and men?"

"You sound as though you don't think that's possible."

"In my experience I haven't found it to be so."

Ariel took a drink of her champagne. "Actually, champagne doesn't loosen me up in the least," she told him, a blatant lie. But she wasn't going to drink enough for him to find out any differently.

"To honesty in art," said Marco, touching her glass with his and waiting while she drank the toast.

"Since you don't believe in honesty between men and women?" she asked him, but instead of answering her he was filling up her glass once again.

The champagne tasted good. Too good. It was insidiously working its way into her system, making her feel relaxed and quite young and very desirable. His eyes never left her, and she didn't think he was faking the warmth she felt in his look. She did keep in mind, however, that they were in a well-lit glass room and clearly visible to the other guests. Which was somewhat reassuring. He wouldn't possibly try anything under the watchful eyes of his guests, would he?

He sat down on the arm of her chair and rested his elbow on the back, his hand playing with the hair above her ear in a way that counteracted the relaxing effect of the wine. She felt herself tense, then forced her muscles to relax. Nothing was going to happen; there was no reason to start getting nervous. Then he leaned down and began to blow softly in her ear, and she quickly revised her thinking and even found herself wondering if Marco got some perverted pleasure out of seducing a woman in a well-lit room with an audience just beyond the glass. Not that his blowing in her ear was doing anything for her. On the contrary, it merely tickled and she found it rather annoying. She moved her head away and gave him a warning glance.

"Something bothering you?" he asked her in a low voice, a voice obviously intended to be sexy so that she was hard put not to laugh aloud.

"It's a little public in here, Marco."

"Ah, is that all that's troubling you?" He stood and reached for her hand. "Come. We will take a walk along the beach."

He gently pulled her to her feet and removed the champagne glass from her hand. *Now you've done it*, she scolded herself. *Now he thinks you want to be alone with him*. And perhaps she did. She was beginning to feel a bit muddled about how she felt about Marco. There was clearly an attraction there. The question was, did she want to do anything about it?

Marco didn't appear to be as indecisive in his feelings. He switched off the light, leading her out the door and down a flight of steep stone steps that wound around rock formations on the way to the beach. He held her hand firmly, steadying her as she placed her feet carefully on each step in order not to catch a heel in one of the crevices.

Well, I can't complain about the lack of privacy, she thought as she viewed the deserted beach. The moon was out, turning the water to silver, making the location as romantic a setting as she could possibly wish for. That is, if she were thinking in terms of romantic settings, which she definitely was not.

She stopped and pulled her hand free, then reached down to remove her sandals, carrying them by the straps in one hand while her free hand once again found his, and they walked side by side down the wet, hard-packed sand at the ocean's edge. At one point he dropped her hand and put his arm around her waist, but Ariel had always found it awkward to walk that way, and moved out of his reach before once again reaching for his hand. Holding hands was nice. Innocent. A hand at the waist, however, could easily wander.

She stole a sidelong glance at him and saw that his eyes were still on her, his expression not easily read in the moonlight. "What are we doing out here, Marco?" she ventured, thinking they must have walked at least half a mile by now.

"I know what I'm doing, but you seem to have your doubts." His hand applied pressure on hers and she felt herself quicken the pace.

"I think maybe we should go back."

She heard a deep chuckle. "I think maybe you don't know what you want, but perhaps I can show you."

She was about to protest that she didn't really want to be shown anything, but then he was stopping and moving around in front of her so that his head blotted out the moonlight, and it was only a dark blur that was moving down at the same time his arms went quite forcefully around her, drawing her body against his just a split second before his lips found hers and she found herself very close to being engulfed in passions that she wasn't very sure she could control.

"Please don't," she tried to say, but his mouth was in the process of prying hers open and it came out a garbled moan that he seemed to take for heightened passion, and the words were a lie anyway. She wanted to see what it would be like to kiss him, to see if any attractive man could turn her on or whether it was something special about Scott.

The experiment was not a success.

It wasn't that she didn't enjoy the kiss. It was just that kissing on public beaches made her nervous, and her eyes kept flying open to see if anyone else had come along. The worst would be if Jody suddenly appeared with some of the other children and found her mother on the beach kissing a strange man. She just couldn't relax and enjoy it, even though his kisses were a delight in themselves, being practiced and of an extremely good quality.

And all this analysis of the situation was doing nothing more than getting her out of the mood, anyway, and any brief effects the champagne might have had had long since dissipated. She was left feeling just slightly ridiculous. When Marco began to ease her slowly down onto the beach, all she could think about was that she was wearing a white jumpsuit and how she couldn't possibly return to the party with it soiled. That thought was the final straw, and she managed to push herself out of his arms and face him sheepishly.

"I'm sorry, it's just no good," she muttered, wishing just once she could act in a more sophisticated manner with a man.

"No good?" His voice sounded incredulous, as though never before had anyone suggested to Marco that his kisses were anything less than expert.

"I don't mean you, you're fine, it's just that it's so public here and..."

He stood back from her and looked around. "We're the only ones on the beach."

"Yes, but there's always the possibility...."

"You were married a very long time?"

"Yes. Yes, I was."

"You're used to the marital bed, the privacy—the sex at night with all the lights out and the children safely in bed."

She smiled ruefully. "I suppose I am."

He sighed deeply. "Marriage always manages to take the spontaneity out of love."

"The kiss of death," she murmured.

"Exactly." He started off down the beach in the direction they had come, but this time didn't take her hand. She found he was making her feel guilty for some unaccountable reason.

"I'm sorry, Marco," she found herself murmuring.

Again he sighed. "Your eyes held such promise. I've seldom been so wrong about a woman."

Had her eyes held promise? Of course they had, she'd been flirting with him outrageously, flattered that yet another attractive man had found her desirable. She really was in danger of losing her dignity if she continued such wanton behavior. It wasn't that the kiss had been such a big deal, but she knew that had the privacy been there it would have progressed far beyond a kiss. Ever since that night with Scott, her body had been eager for more sex. And all it seemed to take was another sexy artist to turn her on.

She felt embarrassed as she crossed the patio behind Marco and saw Jody and some of the other kids engrossed in a card game. At least Jody didn't look up and catch her mother's sheepish look as she returned to the party with Marco.

Scott looked up when she entered the living room, though, and merely gave her a speculative glance before returning his attention to a magnificently attractive woman in an Indian sari who appeared to have gathered a crowd of admirers around her. The woman was clearly older than Ariel, with deeply etched lines around her eyes and mouth, and yet she was exuding the kind of magnetism that drew women as well as men to her side. She was dark with carelessly graying hair and used her hands with small birdlike motions as she spoke to the group.

Ariel felt herself drawn into the crowd and took a

seat on the floor where, on closer investigation, the woman was discoursing on a particular problem she had encountered while working with a piece of marble. So she sculpted, thought Ariel, leaning forward in order to hear the woman better.

When Ariel finally thought to glance at her watch it was past two in the morning, and she realized she would get virtually no sleep that night, in addition to having kept Jody up far past her usual bedtime. She reluctantly got to her feet and headed for the patio but was intercepted halfway there by Scott, who took her by her arm and led her out to the kitchen of the house.

Still holding onto her arm, he leaned back against the counter filled with dirty glasses and gave her a measured look. "So how'd you get along with Marco?" he asked.

"He's very nice," she said lamely, knowing that nice didn't begin to describe anyone, let alone Marco. As he continued to stare at her, making her feel guilty beyond reason, she changed the subject abruptly by asking who the woman was in the living room.

He raised one brow. "That's Juliana, Marco's wife."

"His wife?"

He nodded.

"I didn't know he was married."

"Would it have made a difference?"

"Of course it would have made a difference!"

He gave her a disbelieving look before pulling her over against him. "Don't worry about it. Juliana's quite used to Marco's little affairs."

Ariel couldn't imagine a marriage that entailed being "used to" your husband's affairs. "Well, I hope she's having a good time too," she said, not being a proponent of the double standard.

"Oh, I think I can assure you of that," he murmured, leading her to wonder if he was speaking from personal experience.

She almost asked him, but then thought better of it. And it wasn't any of her business. Yet, she hoped the answer would be yes. It would show that Scott was interested in women of any age and that she wasn't just an eccentricity of the moment for him.

She wished now she hadn't taken the precipitous walk on the beach with Marco. After the night in Mexico with Scott, she had immediately repaired to a singles' party, and now this. He would think of her as a flighty, middle-aged woman on the prowl, and that wasn't the way she wanted to be viewed by him.

"When are we going to see each other again, Ariel?" he was saying to her, and she looked up at him and saw that as foolish as she had been, he still seemed to be interested.

She shrugged. "I don't have much free time."

He put his hands on her shoulders. "Then you still want to see me?"

She nodded, noting that she didn't in the least mind the lack of privacy when it came to Scott. The fact that people were coming in and out of the kitchen didn't even bother her, although the two of them weren't really doing anything, just standing close and looking into each other's eyes.

"What about tomorrow night?"

"I don't know. The girls—"

"Get a sitter if you have to, but let's get together. I'd like you to see where I live. I'll even cook dinner for you, and that's not an invitation to take lightly. I hate cooking!"

"You don't need to—"

"I know I don't need to. I want to."

"All right."

She started to turn to leave, but he leaned down and kissed her before she could move, a teasing kiss that left her with a promise of what was to come the following night. She put her fingers gently to his lips, then turned to find Jody.

Late hour or not, Jody was having a good time, and it was only when Ariel pleaded her own tiredness that her daughter reluctantly followed her out to the car.

"It was neat there, Mom, can we go back some-time?"

"We'll see."

"You always say 'We'll see.' Can't you ever say yes?"

Ariel found she'd like to return, too. Instead of wasting so much time with Marco, she wished now she'd got to know his far more interesting wife. And yet if Marco and Scott were friends, as they appeared to be, perhaps she would see them again sometime. It would be nice to have friends like that, friends with something in common instead of the business friends she and Jack had always entertained during their marriage. They had always been Jack's friends, never hers.

And quite naturally that led her to wonder on the long drive back, with Jody asleep in the back seat, what marriage to Scott would be like. The entire subject was unproductive, of course, since Scott considered marriage the kiss of death. And she wasn't enthusiastic about the subject, either.

And yet what a very different kind of marriage it would be than what she had known. She thought of the two of them painting together, maybe sharing the same studio. They'd get up early in the morning, have coffee, then spend their days together painting. In the evenings they'd either stay home and entertain friends, friends who shared their interests, or perhaps visit other artists in the area. And the nights. The nights would be long, blissful nights of making love, then afterward talking of everything under the sun.

There was only one small hitch to such idle daydreaming. She happened to have a shop to run and two daughters to raise, and somehow neither of those factors lent themselves to such romantic fantasies. Reality would be she'd be working hard in the shop while Scott was whiling away the daylight hours in his studio, wherever it was. Evenings for the most part would be spent supervising the girls, making sure homework got done, all the other tasks necessary to bring up children. And the long nights of love? Well, of necessity they wouldn't be all that long. They couldn't even begin until the girls were safely asleep for the night, and they couldn't last too late or she wouldn't be able to get them up for school in the morning.

Idle speculation, all of it, and to project a simple dinner with him into some idealized marriage was the kind of foolishness she generally avoided. And yet what else was there to think about on the long drive home, when her eyes threatened to close if she didn't think about something interesting enough to keep her awake.

As an alternative, Ariel turned on the car radio and spent the rest of the trip home singing along to the mellow music of the sixties.

Chapter Eleven

The poor, starving artist turned out to have a house on the waterfront in the most exclusive section of Seal Beach. Granted, the winter's rain had managed to erode part of the retaining wall that divided the sand from the back of the property, but he considered himself lucky that that was all the damage done during a year when houses in other beach areas, notably Malibu, had sunk into the sea.

It was with a homeowner's pride that Scott led her around the outside of the house as soon as they arrived. She had time to note the Mercedes parked in the garage alongside his disreputable bike as he headed around the side of the house to show her his private view of the beach and the Pacific.

She was awed and jealous at the same time. She no longer had any desire for a house to take care of, but any structure on beachfront property filled her with aspiration. The back of the house was terraced with several levels of patio, and he seated her in a chaise longue on one level before handing her a strawberry margarita and going back to tend the coals on the barbeque.

A morose-looking dog crawled out from beneath

some bushes and arranged himself at her feet. While scratching him behind his ears, Ariel took in the incredible view of the ocean and what remained of the Seal Beach Pier, one of her favorite spots before the devastating winter storms had destroyed the middle section. The restaurant at the end of the pier was still there, but there was no longer a way to get to it. To her right the sun was edging its way down to the horizon, and she knew that soon she'd be treated to a spectacular sunset, the kind only Southern California had.

"What do you think of it?" Scott asked her, and she knew he was referring to his residence rather than the view.

"I think you're a fraud, that's what!"

"Would you really prefer me to be an indigent artist? I know it sounds romantic, but in reality..."

"Yeah, I know. In reality it's nice to eat."

"You do notice you're getting steak and not hamburger."

She had noticed, all right, and was thrilled by the prospect.

"Still, you might have warned me."

He chuckled. "I wanted you to love me for myself, not my worldly possessions."

"At the moment all I love you for is your body," she teased him.

"That just shows excellent taste on your part."

She turned around to make a face at him and for the first time got a look at the back of the house, or rather the front as it faced the ocean. It was all glass with an arched roof that would give the same light as skylights. She was sure that was where he painted and couldn't wait to see it.

"Can I go inside and look around?"

He shook his head. "The inside tour comes after dinner."

She contented herself with sipping her drink and watching the waves break. Scott put the steaks on, then came and sat beside her.

"Did you tell the girls you were coming over here?"

She gave him a rueful smile. "I didn't have the guts. I just said we were going out to dinner."

"Does that mean you have to be home early?"

"Not too early. I can always say we saw a movie afterward."

"Don't trust them with the truth, huh?"

"What was I supposed to say, Scott, that I was coming over here to make love with you?"

"Is that why you came over?"

"You know very well that's why!"

He sighed. "What do they think their father's doing for a social life?"

"That's different; they don't seem to care what he does. It's me they're protective of."

"So the subterfuge begins."

"I really don't like lying to them, but what choice do I have? I don't think kids can handle having a promiscuous mother."

"You consider being with me promiscuous?" He got up to turn over the steaks, and the smell of the sizzling meat was rendering her ravenous.

"I don't, but they would."

"Maybe it's time they learned what a loving relationship entails."

She looked over at him in surprise. "I don't consider this a loving relationship."

He stopped still, one steak dangling from a long fork. "What do you consider it?"

"Well, you know... a brief affair, I suppose. At first I considered it a one-nighter, but..."

To her consternation Ariel saw that Scott looked insulted by her words, and she wished she'd been more politic. But good heavens, he couldn't be thinking it was any more than that, could he? After all, he was of the younger generation who took sex more casually than she had been brought up to take it.

"That's all it is to you?" The steak was safely on the barbeque and he came back to stare down at her.

What was he complaining about? He seemed to want the affair. "What would you call it, if not an affair?"

"I don't mind the word 'affair,' I think it's 'brief' I object to. I think 'love affair' sounds better, don't you?"

She laughed nervously. "Well, yes, it sounds better. I just wouldn't call it accurate."

"You're beginning to annoy me, Ariel. I think we better change the subject."

She was astonished that he was taking it so seriously. "This is hardly the great love affair of the century, Scott!"

"It couldn't possibly be, not with your attitude!"

"What do you mean my attitude? I thought I had acquired your attitude, which I would think would please you. You're the one who got me to take sex less seriously, or had you forgotten?"

"Yeah, but that was just to get you in bed."

"I was aware of that." Her words were cool.

"I just thought things had changed since then, that's all."

She sighed. "The only thing that's changed is that we know each other more intimately now."

He reached down and took the glass from her hand, placing it on the table, then took her hands and pulled her to her feet. "I don't think that's the only thing," he murmured, putting his arms around her.

She was feeling warm, as she always did when he was close. "Let's not analyze it to death, Scott."

"Don't you ever give any deep thought to anything, Ariel? I'm just trying to say that when I saw you go down to the beach with Marco, I knew things were more serious than I'd thought."

"That was just male ego," she said, lifting her face to his and wishing he'd stop talking long enough to kiss her. Didn't he know there were moments for talk and moments for action, and that this was one of the latter?

"All right, belittle my feelings—"

"I'm not trying to belittle your feelings. I just think there are better ways of expressing them than talk, that's all." He still wasn't getting the message, so she reached up and pulled his head down to hers, and once their lips touched he seemed to get the idea.

And what a good kisser he was, she thought as she moved her body seductively close to his, amazed at how aroused she became at the mere touch of his tongue against her own. They stood there for long moments as their mouths mingled and her temperature seemed to soar to a record high.

He finally broke it off and looked down at her. "Come on, I think it's time to show you the house."

Ariel looked over at the barbeque. "What about the steaks?"

"To hell with the steaks!"

She looked at him in horror. "You mean you don't want to eat first?"

"Do you?"

She nodded. "I haven't had a steak in ages, Scott. And it looks so good, and that smell..."

He gave a sigh of exasperation. "First you want to make love instead of talk, now you want to eat instead of making love. Aren't you ever consistent?"

She shrugged. "I want it all."

His arms went to his sides. "All right, finish your drink and I'll bring the rest of the food out."

She carried her drink over to where he'd set the wrought iron table for two. What was the point of hurrying things when there were two, thick, delicious-looking steaks just waiting to be eaten? Giving in to passions of the moment was fine, but she also had a passion for good food.

He brought out two baked potatoes and a bowl filled with tossed salad, then served their steaks as she poured from the bottle of wine he'd set previously on the table. She saw that he was a little upset with her, but figured the food would cheer him up. It was certainly going to cheer her up!

He didn't say much while they ate, which was all right with her. She was used to eating with two children who rarely stopped talking while they ate, which sometimes made for poor digestion. And anyway, she was afraid if they talked they'd argue, which just might force her to get up and leave before the good part.

"Enjoying the food?" His voice sounded amused.

"Oh, yes—it's wonderful." Well, he wasn't totally silent, but nothing wrong with a little polite conversation over a meal.

"I admire the way you can just turn your emotions on and off like that."

From the sound of his voice she didn't think he admired it at all. "It just seemed like a shame to waste the dinner."

"Wouldn't do to let your feelings overwhelm you, even for a moment. Am I right?"

She gave him a belligerent look. "Are you trying to start a fight?"

"I'm just trying to figure you out, that's all."

"Look, we're not kids. I certainly see nothing wrong in being able to keep my emotions under control."

"Is that what happened between you and Marco? Did he turn out to be too spontaneous for you?"

"That's none of your business!" And the words hit a little too close to the mark.

"Look, I don't give a damn what happened between you and Marco. I'm just trying to figure out how you think, that's all."

"I think you're making a big production over the fact that I thought it would be a shame to waste all this food, that's all. And, if you want the truth, your kisses didn't overwhelm me to the point where I forgot about everything else." She was sure she'd done it now. His next move would probably be to send her home. Fed, but not satisfied.

Instead, he laughed. "Does anything overwhelm you, Ariel?"

She thought back to their night of sex, feeling her face flush at the memory. "You can be pretty overwhelming at times."

"Thanks for the compliment. I think."

She swallowed her last morsel of steak and drank

some wine. The dinner had been perfect, just what she needed. Now if he felt in need of a little after-dinner exercise, she wouldn't protest; in fact, she'd encourage it.

He got up and disappeared into the house with their plates. When he returned he was carrying bowls filled with strawberries and whipped cream. She hadn't thought she could eat another thing, but this looked too tempting to resist.

He lit a cigarette before starting in on his dessert and looked over to where the sun was beginning to set. "You've got to admit I tried. The setting's a little more romantic than Tijuana, wouldn't you say?"

"Definitely more romantic." And the food was better, too.

"Is it getting you in the mood?"

"I was already in the mood."

"Not so that you'd notice."

"Come on, Scott, I don't just turn it on and off, despite what you may think. I just thought we ought to eat dinner first, that's all."

"Tell me something, Ariel. What do you want out of this relationship?"

She swallowed a strawberry before answering. It seemed to be interrogation time again. "Do you have to call it a relationship?"

"All right, what do you want out of this brief affair?"

"Look, Scott, you made it clear from the start that all you wanted was sex. So why don't we just leave it at that?"

"That's all you're interested in?"

"I'm not putting you down, Scott. I enjoy talking to

you—usually. I enjoy arguing with you, sex with you, painting with you..."

"But you enjoy the sex the most."

She could feel her lips tightening in anger. "You couldn't wait to get me to bed. Now you act like it's some kind of crime because I enjoy it. What the hell is it that you want, Scott?"

"I just want you to admit that this is more than sex."

"All right, it's more than sex! It was also a good meal."

"But you don't give a damn for me personally."

"Scott, if I liked impersonal sex I'd be having it with everyone."

"It looked like that was your intention Saturday night."

"And maybe my only mistake Saturday night was not staying down on the beach with Marco!"

His eyes narrowed. "You mean that?"

"At the moment, yes!"

He pushed the bowl of strawberries away from him and she saw they were going to go to waste. Still, she didn't think it was the right moment to reach for them herself. "Let's not argue, Ariel."

"I had no intention of arguing. You just seem to want to talk everything to death."

"Is that how it seems to you?"

She nodded.

"I guess you're right. It's better left for afterward when you've mellowed."

She would have thought good food would also have a mellowing effect, but tonight that wasn't the case. Well, it wasn't too late. It was still a romantic setting, and the sun was now turning the sky into shades of orange and red and pink while mild ocean breezes caressed her skin. And Scott was looking exceptionally appealing in white ducks and a pale blue knit shirt that set off his tan. She was only wearing jeans and a casual blouse herself, but she hadn't wanted the girls to get the idea that tonight was anything special. She gave him what she hoped was a sweet smile as she lifted one of his strawberries out of the bowl.

"All we need to complete the setting," he was saying, "is to have Jody crawl out from behind one of the bushes and aim her rifle at us."

"Don't even think it!"

He chuckled. "I find her amusing."

"I usually do, too, but not in this setting."

He stood up and began gathering up the dishes. "You want another drink while I clean up?"

"Why don't you just leave it until later."

He cocked one brow. "You suddenly in a hurry, Ariel?"

"You going to play games now, Scott?"

"No games. I just think we ought to take it slow and easy."

And pay me back for wanting to eat first, she thought to herself as he disappeared into the house. One thing was for sure: The age difference wasn't bothering her at the moment. Tonight they seemed to be acting equally childishly.

She slid down in her chair and leaned her head back, feeling full and relaxed and quite good. She was sure he'd return from the kitchen quickly; he must be as eager as she was to repair to the bedroom and get down to the good stuff. God, how nice it would be if it could be a regular occurrence instead of having to be sandwiched in between her gallery and the girls and the show and all the other things that were required of her. That was one thing to be said for marriage: You got all the sex without any of the hassle involved. They seemed, at least, to have circumvented the dating part. She probably would have refused if he'd asked her to go to a movie. Movies she could see with the girls.

She kept checking her watch, wondering what was taking him so long. Was he the kind of meticulous housekeeper who was out there washing each dish individually, then drying it and putting it in its proper place? Had their conversation made him lose interest? Or was he simply teasing her? She thought that was probably the answer, and in a way she realized she deserved it. But she wasn't a kid who let her emotions get out of control, that had been proved on the beach with Marco. She could wait until the time was right for sex and then enjoy it. And at the moment the time was right, and where was Scott?

Forget about sitting around and waiting until he thought the time was right. Ariel got up and headed for the sliding glass doors. Once inside, she saw she was indeed in his studio, and her jealousy knew no bounds. Even with the sun almost gone, the room provided more light than she had in the back of her shop with the inadequate fluorescent lighting. Three massive studio easels were placed strategically to catch the light, and the supply of paints and canvases he had on hand rivaled that of an art supply store.

She walked around, admiring everything. She noticed stereo components on a shelf to provide music while he painted, and she began to find it no wonder he did such good work. Not that he didn't have the talent, but if she had a place like this to paint she'd never want to leave it for a moment. And he was meticulously neat, it seemed. Everywhere she looked everything was in its place, and there wasn't even signs of splattered paint on the floor.

Which, no doubt, accounted for his being in the kitchen for so long. Maybe the fool was mopping the floor!

Two steps led up to another room, and she found herself in what must be the living room, enormously long with a stone fireplace and a view of the Pacific. It was filled with comfortable-looking leather furniture and again was unnervingly spotless. Well, he didn't have two kids to clean up after. If she lived alone, she was sure she could manage to be that neat, too.

Off the living room was a formal dining room, and beyond that she at last spotted the kitchen. But instead of mopping the floor, Scott was leaning on the counter and drinking a beer.

"Were you planning on having me wait all night?"

He turned around with a smile. "I didn't think a little anticipation would hurt."

"A little wouldn't, but enough is enough."

He set down his beer and held out his hand. "Come on, I'll show you the bedroom."

"Maybe I'd like a beer."

"As you said, enough is enough." He took her hand and she didn't protest as he led her down a carpeted hallway and into a bedroom where the first thing that caught her eye was the enormous mirrored wall behind the equally enormous bed.

"A little tacky," she murmured.

"But not my tackiness. The previous owner put it in."

"And you just left it."

He was eyeing them both in the mirror. "Would you like me to cover it with a sheet?"

She shook her head as though disinterested. Actually, she was thinking it might be interesting to be able to watch in the mirror as they made love. She watched his image in the mirror as he turned to her and took her in his arms. She melted against him, her desire once again surfacing. And this time she would let herself be overwhelmed by it.

Ariel found herself peering over his shoulder at their mirror images as he slowly unbuttoned her blouse and let it fall to the floor, moving next to the front clasp on her bra. The sight of his deeply tanned hands against the white of her breasts excited her as much as his touch. He reached to remove his own shirt, and then her hands moved to undo the buckle at the same time his hands were unbuttoning her jeans.

Very quickly they were both on the bed, and she was no longer able to see them in the mirror as his body covered hers and he was moving to enter her with an eagerness she shared. It felt good and natural and very, very right with Scott, she couldn't help thinking as their bodies fit together and their rhythms synchronized. And now that she was experiencing the same ecstasy she had felt the first time she'd been with him, she wondered why the steak dinner had ever seemed that important. This was surely more satisfying than steak.

Raising himself on his hands between thrusts he

paused, looking down at her with eyes darkened by passion. "Is sex all it really is, Ariel?"

Her eyes implored him to continue; much too excited to speak, she tried to pull him down, but he stubbornly stayed where he was, waiting for her reply.

"Well? Is it? Is that all that's between us?"

She shook her head, hoping that would satisfy him and he'd continue. Her body moved seductively beneath his, but he remained still.

"Say it, Ariel; say I mean more to you than that."

"You mean more to me than that, Scott," she muttered, giving in to the emotional blackmail in order to get on with the pleasure.

He hesitated a moment longer as though waiting for more, then once again took up the rhythm where he'd left off. She found herself wondering why he'd paused for the exchange. Perhaps in payment for her postponing the sex, she thought, and then all thought ceased as she felt her body begin to build toward the moment it was all leading up to. She heard herself cry out just before his body came to a shuddering stop on top of her, and they clung together, their breath ragged until Scott rolled off to lie beside her and take her in his arms.

"Was that pause in there necessary?" she asked him when he reached for his cigarettes on the bedside table.

"I thought so."

"It didn't prove anything. I would have told you almost anything at that moment."

"I'm aware of that. I just find it rather disconcerting to make love with such a silent woman."

She pondered his words. "I'm not any good at talking sexy in bed," she finally said.

He chuckled. "I don't need that kind of talk."

She frowned. "I don't think Jack and I ever said much when we made love."

"I don't want to hear about it."

"I'm just mentioning a fact, that's all. I think all he ever said was, 'Are you ready?' and then I'd either nod or shake my head."

"Sounds very romantic."

"Maybe it was different in the beginning, but it's hard to remember."

"It looks as though I have a few more things to teach you."

She smiled over at him. "Teach away."

"Give me a minute and I will."

Her hand moved to nestle among the hair on his chest as she looked around his bedroom, noticing the details for the first time. One entire wall looked as if it consisted of closets, and a low triple dresser was against one wall. Beneath the windows was a table and two chairs, a perfect spot for a midnight snack.

"How many bedrooms do you have?" she asked him.

"Why, are you interested in trying them all?"

"I was just wondering."

"Just wondering if there's room for your two daughters?"

She removed her hand and folded her arms across her chest. "I wasn't wondering any such thing!"

He laughed. "It's okay, there's two more, one for each of them, and we can share."

She gave him a suspicious look. "Are you inviting us to move in with you?"

"I don't know what I'm doing."

"That's what I thought."

He reached over to pull her close. "But it's always a possibility."

"Just what you need, three females moving in on you and destroying your life-style."

"I know a lot of guys who'd love having three females move in with them."

"Very funny!"

"I thought it was."

As he stubbed out his cigarette in the ashtray, she pushed him down on the bed and climbed on top of him. From this position she could see them both quite clearly in the mirror. The indirect lighting in the bedroom was very flattering, and she thought they looked very good together in bed. Even sitting up and leaning over him, as she was now doing, she didn't sag in the least, and her stomach was as firm as a girl's.

"Admiring yourself?" he asked her.

She tore her eyes away from the mirror. "Don't be ridiculous!"

"You should be admiring yourself. You have a great body."

Yeah, for an old lady, she thought, making a face at the thought.

"It would be even greater if you started moving it," he suggested.

She saw with delight that he was ready again, and she lifted herself and then moved down on top of him, gasping with pleasure at the deep penetration. She began to move, very slowly at first in order to prolong the pleasure, watching herself surreptitiously in the mirror part of the time and the rest of the time watching the reactions on Scott's face. This was a position Jack had never favored, having some outmoded idea that the man should be on top, and she began to see why it was that so many men did seem to have that idea. It was no doubt because it was more fun on top; she found she enjoyed being the one setting the pace.

On the other hand, she didn't seem to have his control. She was soon moving up and down much faster than she had planned, and when she felt herself nearly bursting inside, she couldn't even keep up the motion, but moved to cover his body with her own, leaving him to do the finishing from beneath. She heard him murmur, "My love, my love," in her ear, but she was too engrossed in the sensations spreading over her body to pay much attention.

"I wish you could stay the night," he said to her when they were once more relaxing side by side.

She looked at her watch and saw that she should leave soon. "I wish I could, too, but..."

"How about tomorrow night, can you get out?"

"I don't see how—that's a little soon." She felt as if she were a teenager plotting how to get out of the house.

"Wednesday?"

"I have my class with your mother."

"I can see now this isn't going to be a satisfactory arrangement."

She was beginning to see it, too. Maybe Jack would take the girls for the summer. And what kind of mother was she, planning how to get rid of her daughters just so she could enjoy some steady sex? "What nights are you going to be down at the festival?"

"I suppose whatever nights I can't see you."

"You'd rather see me?"

"Hell, yes!" He pulled her close. "Why do you look so surprised?"

"Don't you see anyone else? Any other women?"

"Not since meeting you."

"Why not?"

"You're an intelligent woman, Ariel. I would think you could figure that one out for yourself."

She sat up on the side of the bed. "I think I better get home."

"Conversation getting too serious for you?"

She reached for her clothes on the floor, then carried them into the bathroom. The conversation was getting too serious, and so, she thought, was Scott. The nice little affair she thought she was embarking on was turning into more than that, and this was something she didn't think she could handle. She didn't want words like "love" to intrude. She had assumed he would be able to keep everything on the casual level she wanted, because if it was up to her she knew it wouldn't take much for her to fall completely in love with him.

When she left the bathroom he was already dressed. "I'll drive you home," he told her.

"I can walk, Scott."

"We can both walk." His voice seemed to brook no argument, and she guessed she should have him see her home, since her daughters had seen her leave with him. It was the kind of thing she expected from Nicole's dates, after all, so there was no reason to set a bad example.

He took her hand as they left the house and headed toward Main Street. "When do you think you can see me again?" he asked.

"I don't know. I just can't leave Jody alone all the time."

"Bring her along tomorrow night; we can have a picnic on the beach."

"But if I bring her along..."

"In other words, you really do only want to see me for sex."

"You mean you wouldn't mind if we couldn't?"

"Of course I wouldn't mind. I do enjoy your company, you know, and I also enjoy Jody."

"Kids can be—"

"Don't tell me about kids, you've seen where I grew up. I miss having all those people around."

"All right, but only if I'm allowed to bring the picnic. I can't have you cooking for me all the time."

All was quiet when they reached the apartment, and Scott went in with her while she checked on the kids. She was glad they were asleep already, as she didn't feel up to being questioned about why dinner had taken so long.

"Tomorrow night, then?" Scott confirmed at the door.

"I might bring along Nicole, too, if she wants to come."

"Fine, she can even bring her boyfriend."

"Maybe you'd like Jack along, too."

He laughed softly. "Children, yes—ex-husbands, no."

He leaned down to kiss her, and she found herself wanting very much to go back to his house with him instead of being left to sleep alone on the couch.

Once in bed she allowed herself to think about what it would be like to live with Scott. Despite never having wanted a house to care for again, she knew it was an inducement. Right now, while she was trying to sleep in a stuffy apartment, he was no doubt feeling cool ocean breezes on his body. Jody and Nicole wouldn't have to share a room, she'd have someone to talk to, to paint with. And best of all, someone to sleep with at night.

But even thinking about it was rushing things. She couldn't claim to know him that well in so brief a time, and she still couldn't believe he'd want to saddle himself with an older woman with two daughters who would completely disrupt his life. He was thinking with his body now, not his brain, and when the novelty of their lovemaking wore off he'd no doubt come to his senses.

She only hoped the same could be said of her.

Chapter Twelve

"It's not working out!" Ariel wailed.

"What do you mean?" asked Sutton. "You seem to be positively blooming."

"I'm constantly being put in the position of lying to my daughters, and I get the feeling I'm not fooling them in the least. Scott and I have to keep sneaking around like teenagers, we never seem to have enough time together, and worst of all—I think I've fallen in love."

"I could have told you that weeks ago."

Ariel buried her face in her arms. "Love is for the young, Sutton. This whole affair is wearing me out!"

"So marry him."

"I like him too much to do that to him."

"Very noble sentiments, but the man's obviously besotted with you. Anyway, there's nothing like marriage to calm the emotions."

"I know—I keep thinking that. But I don't want what we have to turn into what I had with Jack."

"You were happy with Jack."

"Yes, but never ecstatic."

"I think that has more to say about Scott than about

marriage. Listen, Ariel, despite all my talk to the contrary, if I found some guy who made me ecstatic, I'd get married again."

"For one thing, he's never asked me."

"With your attitude, he's probably afraid to try. No one looks for rejection, you know."

"My daughters would—"

"Your daughters would love it! Nicole's crazy about his house and Jody's crazy about him."

"Do you know Jody's taken to following us?"

"How do you know?"

"We see her. Every time I say I'm going somewhere with Scott, we catch sight of her running behind buildings or hiding beneath bushes to see where we're going."

"Where are you going?"

"Usually to his house, but when we see her we end up going for ice cream or a drink. It really is wearing me out."

"The only way you're going to normalize the relationship is to move in with him."

"My daughters wouldn't approve of my living in sin."

"An antiquated notion these days, but you're probably right. That's why you have to get married."

"I swore I'd never get married again."

"Yes, well, we all say things that quickly change under the right circumstances."

"He thinks marriage is the kiss of death."

"Does he still say that?"

"No, but he said it when we met."

"I don't know what to tell you, Ariel, but it doesn't look to me as if those are still his sentiments."

"Just supposing I did want to marry him, Sutton, what should I do? He's never even mentioned the word since his 'kiss of death' speech."

"Bring it up—subtly, of course."

"And just how do I do that?"

"You're intelligent—you'll think of a way."

"Are you and Scott going to get married, Mom?"

It was Jody speaking, but both girls were watching her, waiting for her reply. "Eat your breakfast, Jody."

"Well, Mom—I think we're entitled to know!"

Nicole was attempting to look unconcerned as she put more raspberries on her shredded wheat, but she wasn't fooling Ariel. She was every bit as curious as Jody and she supposed they were both entitled to an answer.

"The subject hasn't come up, honey."

"People don't get married anymore, Jody," Nicole was telling her younger sister. "They just move in together, right, Mom?"

"Some do," admitted Ariel. After all, their father had just moved the Norma Kamali aficionado in with him, so she couldn't very well dispute it.

"You wouldn't do that, would you, Mom?" asked Jody, which made her a very young believer in the double standard, not having said a word about her father's new roommate.

"I have no intention of moving in with anyone," Ariel assured her.

For some reason Jody didn't look relieved. "Does that mean you're not going to marry Scott?"

"The question hasn't come up," Ariel told her.

"She means he hasn't asked her," said Nicole.

Jody reached over and put her hand on her mother's arm. "You want me to talk to him, Mom?"

"I certainly do not!"

"That wouldn't be cool," said Nicole.

"I didn't know you were so anxious to get me married off. We're doing okay, aren't we?"

"I wouldn't mind you marrying Scott," said Jody in a low voice.

Ariel looked over at Nicole, who shrugged indifferently. "Don't look at me, it's your decision."

"Well, I think it's a little early to have this kind of conversation. I've only known him for a few weeks."

"Yeah, but you see him every day."

"I don't see him that often, Jody."

"Name one day lately that you haven't seen him. Just one!"

That was a tough one. They did manage to see each other daily, she realized. "Don't you see your friends every day?"

"Yeah." Reluctantly.

"It would be nice to have a normal life again, though," observed Nicole.

"Normal? What's abnormal about the way we're living?"

"I wouldn't mind having my own room again." Trust Nicole to have noted the number of bedrooms in Scott's house.

"I don't like Scott for his worldly possessions," Ariel informed her. Not that it wouldn't be nice not to have to sleep on the living-room couch anymore.

"I like him for himself, Mom," said Jody. "I like him a lot."

"I know you do, honey—so do I. And I'm perfectly

happy the way things are, so I don't want to hear any
more discussions of marriage. Do you read me?''

"Yeah, Mom."

"Yeah, okay."

"Good. Now who wants to help me with the dishes?"

The age difference no longer seemed of any importance. Ariel wasn't quite sure exactly when or how this
had happened; she only knew the paranoia had gone, at
least for the time being. She attributed it mostly to the
fact that when they were together there just didn't
seem to be any difference. And why should there be?
Four years was hardly monumental. Sutton kept telling
her she'd never looked better, and Ariel saw confirmation of this in the bathroom mirror. Happiness seemed
to make her bloom.

She got to know many of Scott's friends, all of them
artists and of all ages. They saw Marco and Juliana frequently, and Marco didn't seem to hold the episode on
the beach against her. She became quite close with Juliana, and the older woman encouraged her to become
more serious with her work.

Ariel was still attending Rose's classes and going out
on the art show on Sundays, but she thought when the
kids went back to school she'd probably quit both. The
shop was doing well enough so that money was no
longer a big problem, and she took no pleasure in painting pretty florals anymore. Scott had shown her what
she was capable of doing, and now she wanted to
stretch those capabilities to the limit. She thought that
with a lot of serious work for the next two years she
might be able to be considered for the Laguna Beach
Art Fesitival, and she was aiming in that direction.

Things became hectic as Labor Day drew closer and the girls prepared to go back to school. Nicole wanted an entire new wardrobe and planned to pay for part of it herself with the money she'd earned tending shop for Ariel. With both the business on the Mexican frames and the custom framing doing well, she saw no reason why Nicole shouldn't be newly outfitted. The past year Nicole had cheerfully made do with clothes that were both well-worn and out of style. Jody was still in her guerrilla stage, and while it bothered Ariel to have to shop for her daughter in the Army-Navy store, she knew there was no point in investing money in clothes Jody would never put on her back.

On the Sunday before the Labor Day weekend Ariel told her friends on the art show that she was quitting. It wasn't as traumatic a leave-taking as it might have been a few months before, because most of the artists were now buying frames from her and she knew she'd see them often and keep up on the news. And Pat, her closest friend on the show, had agreed to teach a class in seascape painting at her gallery, so she'd see the woman at least once a week.

She hadn't as yet told Rose she was quitting her class, but Scott's mother had invited them to a family barbecue the Saturday of the Labor Day weekend, and Ariel thought she'd tell her then.

On the Friday night before the party, she and Scott were able to have an evening alone as Nicole was taking her younger sister to the movies. Scott made potato salad and they bought take-out fried chicken and had a picnic on the beach in front of his house.

It was the beginning of September, one of Southern California's hottest months, and after they ate it was still warm enough to go in the water, so they changed into their suits and had a swim. The beach was almost deserted except for a few surfers at the other end, and after they swam they lay contented on the blanket and talked for a while.

"I guess the honeymoon's about over," Ariel said during a lull in the conversation. She had never put Sutton's advice into effect, finding no subtle way of bringing up the subject of marriage, but after the words popped out she realized this wasn't a bad way.

"The honeymoon?"

"Figuratively speaking."

"I'm not following you, Ariel," he said, and she almost dropped the subject. Except it was pertinent and he might not realize how radically things were about to change.

"I just mean we're not going to be able to see much of each other anymore, that's all."

"Tired of me already?" His hand reached over to brush her hair out of her eyes and she saw he wasn't taking it seriously.

"You know the kids go back to school this week."

"I would think that'd give us even more time together."

She shook her head. "It won't work out that way. When they're in school I'll be in the shop, and I'm going to have to stay at home with them at night."

"Every night?"

"Every school night. If I'm not there they won't get their homework done or get to bed at a decent hour. I'm pretty free with them during the summer, but school nights are different."

"Does that mean we're reduced to dating on week-

ends like normal people?'' He was still teasing her, and
she didn't think explaining it was going to drive the
point home.

"Maybe Saturday nights. I can't just go off and leave
Jody alone all the time, and Nicole herself will be dating on weekends."

He started to get to his feet. "Then we better take
advantage of every minute we have," he said, reaching
down to help her up.

"Meaning what?"

"Meaning it's time to go inside. From what you're
saying, it may be a long time before I see you again."

"You'll see me tomorrow night."

"Yes, but there's not a whole lot we can do at my
parents' house, unless you're more adventurous than I
think you are."

She wished he hadn't mentioned the party. She was a
little leery about how his family was going to feel when
he brought his grown-up lady friend and her two children to the party. She knew that Rose approved, but
there were a lot of family members she hadn't met as
yet.

Once inside she shed her suit and waited while he
filled the hot tub. She had heard about them but had
never been in one before he suggested it to her one
night. She found it both erotic—at least with Scott in
the tub with her—and relaxing, and now they used it
together at least a couple of times a week.

She slid into the hot, steamy water and leaned her
head back against the side of the tub. Scott got in across
from her, and for a while only their feet touched beneath the water. She was feeling a little disappointed
and a little piqued that Scott hadn't seemed to mind

that they wouldn't be seeing so much of each other anymore. Granted, he probably didn't realize the implications yet, but he could use his imagination, couldn't he? If she had expected him to say immediately, "Well, then we'd better get married, hadn't we?" she'd been very wrong. But then, she hadn't really expected that. Scott seemed perfectly happy with things as they were, and she couldn't really fault him for that.

Ariel was perfectly happy, too, and it was only selfish concerns on her part that made her even think about a change. Selfish concerns like wanting sex regularly with him every night. She seemed to be turning into a sex enthusiast in her old age. She couldn't remember caring whether she and Jack had sex once a night, once a week or once a month, but with Scott she had only to see him to feel the now-familiar stirring in her body.

Which she was feeling now, at the sight of his naked body floating beneath the surface of the hot tub.

He caught the direction of her eyes and grinned. "Be patient, love—it's still early."

She quickly averted her eyes and was glad the heat of the tub masked her flush. "I don't know what you're talking about."

"You know very well what I'm talking about." One of his toes began to move sensuously up and down her leg, and despite the heat she shivered.

"I think I'm turning into a sex maniac, Scott," she admitted.

"Ummm, I've noticed."

"You don't mind?"

He slid down farther into the tub, and his toe was now on the inside of her thigh. "Why should I possibly mind?"

"I don't know—it just doesn't seem proper at my age."

He laughed with pleasure. "I thought you were over your hang-up about your age."

She hadn't even known he knew she had one. "Doesn't it ever bother you?" She was never going to ask that, never put it into words, but they just slipped out.

"Are you referring to the vast age difference between us?"

"Vast?"

He chuckled. "I'm sure at one time you considered it vast. I remember your very quickly pointing out your age to me when we met, as though I gave a damn about a thing like that."

"Doesn't it ever bother you at all?"

"No, I love it! Makes me feel young and sexy."

"Bastard!"

"Come on, Ariel, don't you feel young and sexy when we're together?"

"That's different."

"All right, if you want my considered opinion I'll give it to you. I think if by great luck or fate or whatever, you happen to meet someone in this world who's perfect for you, then a small detail like age shouldn't have any importance at all. And I do consider it pure luck. There aren't a whole lot of people who ever have that happen to them."

"You think I'm perfect for you?"

"Did I say that?"

She kicked water in his face, then turned as he reciprocated.

"Yes, I think you're perfect for me," he told her. "And what's more, I think I'm perfect for you."

A glow of happiness suffused her at his words. She was basking in it when she heard him say, "Well? I don't hear you hastening to agree."

She smiled enigmatically.

"Don't you agree I'm perfect for you?"

"Most of the time."

"What do you mean 'most of the time'? I'm perfect for you all the time."

"Except when you act as if you know everything in the world."

He started toward her across the tub. "I do know everything in the world."

"Oh, really?"

He stood up in the tub, then reached down and lifted her up in his arms. Dripping wet, he stepped out of the tub and headed in the direction of his bedroom.

"Scott, we should dry off first!"

"Don't talk to me as if I were one of your children, love. Anyway, you feel deliciously warm and wet and by the time I'm done with you..."

"Yes?"

He buried his face in her neck and kissed her until she was squirming in his arms. Her hand trailed down his body until it came to rest at his most vital point and she felt him pick up his pace to the bedroom.

He dropped her unceremoniously on the bed before joining her, his mouth closing over hers and his hands moving over her body to leave each touched point quivering in its wake. When he finally entered her, his hands moving to clasp her breasts, she was in the stage of feeling like melted Jell-o and had to leave most of the work to him, gasping with pleasure at each sure stroke.

They remained together spoon-fashion afterward, his breath warm and uneven on her neck. She folded her arms across his and rested contentedly in his arms. And oh, how she was going to miss this near-nightly occurrence.

"You invigorate me, you know that?" he asked. "I feel like I could go on all night."

"Don't let me stop you."

"God, I feel about eighteen."

She rolled out of his arms and faced him. "What were you doing about a sex life before me?" She'd never asked him anything that personal before, but since he never hesitated to question her...

"In retrospect, not a hell of a lot."

"I find that a little hard to believe."

"There was one lady in the spring—very nice—but she began to get a little serious."

Involuntarily, she felt herself stiffen. Was he trying to tell her something? Was she, perhaps, becoming a little too serious and was he trying to warn her off?

He must have read the expression on her face. "My feelings for her weren't that strong, that's all. I thought they might be at first, but it just didn't work out."

She gradually relaxed. She was worrying needlessly. If there was one thing she was sure of, it was that her feelings for Scott were returned in full. He might be leery of marriage, but she was sure he loved her even though the words hadn't been spoken. And she'd be pretty leery of marriage to someone with two kids, too. Being a stepparent, she had heard, was no piece of cake.

She looked at her watch and saw that once again it was time to go home. It seemed as though it were always time to go home. She was always taking off her clothes and then putting them back on and going home to sleep alone in her own bed with no warm arms to hold her close or reach out for her in the morning.

Not that there weren't pluses to the arrangement. She was also free to sleep on as much of her bed as she wanted and not be obliged to be cheerful on the mornings when she wanted nothing more than to cover her head with the sheet and wish that it wasn't time to get up once again.

And yet she thought she'd be happy to forgo those dubious pleasures.

"Ariel, I'm so glad you could make it. And this must be Nicole and Jody." Scott's mother, looking terrific in short-shorts and a tank top, rushed over to greet them. Nicole, who had been allowed to bring her boyfriend along, introduced him to Rose.

Both girls had perked up when they saw the large gathering at Scott's parents' house. Nicole and her friend went over to where some other teenagers were listening to a radio blaring, and Jody soon joined a younger group of children in a volleyball game.

Ariel was led around by Scott and introduced to members of the largest extended family it had ever been her pleasure to meet. Scott had sisters and brothers older than her, her age, and younger, and in addition there were aunts and uncles and cousins and in-laws and even some friends who, he explained, were "just like family."

Scott's father, a small, quiet man who didn't look as

though he had the stamina for such numerous progeny, was off in a corner of the yard playing the flute in a chamber music group, and Scott informed her that his father played with the Los Angeles Symphony Orchestra. All in all, it was an amazing family.

"What an incredibly large family," Ariel murmured to Scott in wonder.

"Makes you wonder how Mom ever had time to paint, doesn't it?"

"It must have been wonderful, growing up with so many people around."

He laughed. "Only those who grew up without brothers or sisters have that reaction. I always envied people I met who were only children. I never knew the meaning of privacy until I moved out."

"Don't you want to have a family of your own like that some day?" She was playing with fire again, but she couldn't help asking.

"Are you crazy? I don't need any children of my own. I have so many nieces and nephews now I can hardly keep them all straight."

Easy to say, but she thought he'd feel differently if they were his own. "It must be wonderful at Christmas." That was one time in her childhood when she'd missed having other children in the family. The focus of attention had always been on her, and she'd always had to be overly enthusiastic over each gift so as not to spoil the day.

"Wonderful? It's a nightmare! My gift list is so long I have to start shopping in September." But he was smiling when he said it, and she knew he probably loved having his family around on holidays.

"Furthermore, have you ever had to wait to use the

bathroom when there were five people lined up in front of you?"

Ariel laughed. "Well, you don't have to worry about that anymore. You have three all to yourself."

"Are you making a social comment on my life-style?"

"No, I'm just envying you. One teenage girl monopolizes the bathroom as much as any other five people put together."

"I heard that, Mother," said Nicole coming up to them. She turned to Scott. "I didn't know Cindi was your sister."

Scott frowned. "Cindi? Oh, Cindi. No, she's my niece."

"You've got a great family," the girl said as she went back to join her crowd.

"I think my family is falling in love with your family," noted Ariel.

"Good, we can take your kids to all the family gatherings and then leave to be by ourselves."

"I like them, too."

"How's my son treating you?" Rose asked her later when the two were alone for a minute.

Ariel still didn't feel at ease with the fact that she was involved with her friend's son. "We're getting along fine."

"No marriage plans yet?" Why was everyone so concerned with her marital state?

"Scott doesn't think artists should be married," said Ariel, hoping that Rose wouldn't ask her what she thought.

"Scott always did have to be told what was good for him," said Rose.

"Well, I hope you aren't going to mention—"

Rose's hands flew up in the air. "Wouldn't think of interfering! Scott's a grown man, he can do what he wants. I still think you two are perfect together, though."

"Would you really want your son married to an older woman with two children?"

"Why not?"

She couldn't think of a suitable reply to that. Why not indeed? Two more children wouldn't even be noticed in this family.

Several of Scott's relatives got around to the same subject, but not as directly as Rose, for whom subtlety was a lost cause. Ariel managed to ignore the inferences and let Scott handle the questions. Not that she thought it was the first time he'd had to parry answers to questions of when he was going to get married. She was sure that every time he brought a new woman to one of the family gatherings, he was opening himself up to the subject.

The abundance of food and drink and the overabundance of new people to meet, plus volleyball when the adults were able to wrest the court from the kids, and dancing later on the patio all combined to tire Ariel to the point where at ten that night she knew she had to get home and get some sleep for her last art show the following day. Nicole wanted to stay on for a while, and Jody had to be literally dragged away from her new friends to accompany her mother home.

Jody went in the apartment ahead of Ariel, who stood outside saying good night to Scott.

"I really enjoyed it," she assured him, her yawns almost extinguishing the words.

He chuckled. "Yeah, they wear me out, too."

"It's just that I have to get up so early...."

He put his arms around her and drew her close. "So when am I going to see you again? You doing anything Labor Day?"

She shook her head. "Jack's taking the girls to Disneyland, more power to him. It's kind of a tradition for them on Labor Day."

"Good, then we'll start our own tradition."

"Doing what?"

"I'll give you one guess," he said before bending down and kissing her.

She thought it sounded like a pretty good tradition to start.

Chapter Thirteen

Luckily, they were on the patio—fully clothed, having a drink. A half hour sooner and they would have still been in bed. A half hour later they might also have been in bed. But at the moment, thank heavens, they were looking as pure as the driven snow, a phrase not often used by Southern Californians, thought Ariel as she caught sight of Jody rounding the house.

It was who was following Jody, right behind Nicole, that made her catch her breath.

"Campbell, you son of a gun, what's this I hear about you carrying on with my daughter?"

My God, thought Ariel, peering into the sun with squinted eyes to see if what she thought she was hearing was really the voice of her father. A father she had thought was hundreds of miles away in Mexico.

"Red Ryan, as I live and breathe," murmured Scott as Ariel hurled herself out of the chair and flew into Red's welcoming arms.

"I thought you said you were going to the fish fry at Sunset Beach," said Nicole in a deceptively innocent voice.

"Yeah, that's what you told us," said Jody. "But when

we looked for you there, no one had seen you. I told Grandpa you'd probably be here. You're always here."

"Why aren't you in Mexico?" she asked her father, standing back to get a good look at him. For the first time in Ariel's memory, her father had a tan and looked positively healthy. He'd even lost the potbelly he'd acquired in recent years. "Marriage certainly seems to agree with you."

"Damn right it does," asserted Red. He looked over to the patio, where Scott was still seated. "I want a few words with you, Scott, but first I'll have one of whatever it is you're drinking."

"We're having margaritas," said Scott, getting to his feet.

Red's face fell. "Forget it. I'll have a beer. If I never see another margarita again, it'll be too soon."

"Where's Christine?" Ariel asked him.

"Dropped her off to say hello to her folks."

"So what are you doing back a year early? Didn't you like Mexico?" If anything, she thought her father would have stayed longer than the designated two years. All her life she'd heard about his dream of going to Mexico to live.

"Mexico was great, but we started to miss everybody." Red took the beer Scott handed him, then patted his flat stomach. "Notice what good shape I'm in?" he asked Ariel.

"I noticed it right away."

"Christine jogs every morning."

"Christine jogs, and you lost the weight?" She wondered if it was possible to lose weight by osmosis.

"Had to go along with her to scare away the lizards. She hates lizards."

Ariel realized she had something in common with her new stepmother: They were both afraid of Mexican lizards.

"How'd the painting go?" Scott asked him.

"Can't wait to show you—got a van full of paintings. Best work I've ever done, if I do say so myself."

"That's great, Red," said Scott with a look of affection for the older man.

"Don't try to butter me up, Campbell. I hear you've been trifling with my daughter's affections, and I want to get to the bottom of this."

Ariel handed Scott her empty glass. "Would you fix me another?"

Scott shook his head. "I can handle your father."

"So can I, but I'd like another drink."

Scott reluctantly went inside and Ariel turned to Red, hands on hips. "Since when are you coming on the concerned father? I'm a grown woman, you know."

"If I thought you'd be interested in Scott, I would have introduced you myself."

"Maybe you should have!"

"Hey, don't get mad at me, honey. Scott's a good guy—good artist. I have nothing against him."

"Then why are you embarrassing me like this?"

"That's between me and Scott."

"No, it isn't!" She turned to the girls, who were avidly listening to the exchange. "Why don't you two take a walk on the beach?"

"You're not getting rid of us that easily," said Jody, and Nicole nodded in agreement.

"What'd I miss?" asked Scott, returning with a refill for Ariel.

"Not a thing," Ariel told him, taking the drink

and sitting back down on the patio. "My father's decided that finally, at age thirty-eight, I need his advice."

Red sat down in a chaise longue and took a pack of crumpled Mexican cigarettes out of his pocket, taking one out and slowly lighting it. "I hear from Rose that you two are an item—her words, not mine."

Ariel looked surprised. "You heard from Rose?"

"Sure, we correspond. Good friend, Rose. And you never told me anything in your letters."

Scott looked amused. "Leave it to my mother...."

"Have you seen the gallery, Dad?" asked Ariel, wishing fervently that they could get off the subject of her and Scott.

"Didn't you get rid of it?"

Ariel shook her head. "I not only kept it, it's making money. Thanks mostly to Scott."

"I've even been working there, Grandpa," said Nicole.

"And Scott lets me sit in on his workshops," added Jody.

"I put in a line of custom framing and some Mexican frames too," Ariel told him. "And I'm going to have different artists teaching classes during the week."

"You're turning into a regular Rose Saunders," said Red with a grin.

Scott laughed out loud. "At least I've gotten your daughter to stop painting florals. You should see what she's doing now—she's really good."

"Damn right. I taught her first," said Red.

"Would you kids like to go get a pizza and bring it back?" Ariel asked them.

"No," they chorused.

"They ought to hear this. It affects their future, too," said Red.

Ariel sighed. "Dad, you're making it sound as though Scott's taken advantage of me somehow. Just look at the facts: I'm older than he is, I'm divorced, I have two kids—"

"Right," said Scott, "she could be the one taking advantage of me."

Ariel laughed. "Exactly!"

"That's not the way I see it," said Red, a mutinous look on his face.

"What are you going to do, Dad, forbid me to see him?" Ariel said with a smile.

"You might think this is funny, young lady, but you have two young daughters—"

"Leave us out of it," Nicole cut in.

"Yeah, we like Scott," said Jody.

Scott looked pretty pleased at that. "Just what's the problem, Red?"

"I just think you two ought to make it legal, and so does your mother."

Ariel was outraged. "You're talking as if we're a couple of high school kids!"

"Yeah," agreed Nicole.

"Anyway, he hasn't asked her," said Jody, getting a withering look from Ariel for her efforts.

Scott addressed Jody. "Are you referring to marriage?"

Jody nodded. "That's what she told us, anyway."

"I'll tell you, Red," said Scott, sitting back in the chair and crossing his legs. "You've got a very independent daughter, who's enjoying her freedom. I think the last thing on her mind is marriage."

Red looked at Ariel. "Is that true?"

Ariel shrugged. "Scott thinks marriage is the kiss of death for artists."

Red looked at Scott. "Is that true?"

Scott spread out his arms. "It's a philosophy I learned at your feet, Red."

Red seemed to ponder this. "It seems to me I did used to say something of the kind. I was wrong, though, Scott—marriage has been great for my painting. In fact, it's been great all around." His eyes took on a dreamy look.

"I'll take your word for that, sir," said Scott, getting a dirty look from Red at the use of the word "sir," "but the fact of the matter is your daughter's not in love with me."

Ariel gave Scott a zero for lack of perception. "Nor is he in love with me," she said, hoping it wasn't true.

Red looked at Scott for confirmation. "Is that true?"

"Not at all—I love your daughter very much. I'm also pretty crazy about your granddaughters, even though they don't know when it's time to take a walk on the beach."

The girls ignored the hint.

"Then why didn't you ever tell me?" Ariel gave Scott an outraged look.

"You should've known!"

"How was I supposed to know when you never said anything?"

Red got to his feet. "You guys got twenty minutes to solve this. I'm taking the girls for pizza."

Ariel and Scott waited in silence until they heard a car start up before she turned on him. "It would have been nice if you'd told me just once when we were making love!"

"I could say the same for you!"

"I was thinking it, at least!"

"So was I!"

Ariel folded her arms across her chest and shoved out her lower lip.

"Come on, now," said Scott. "Don't act like Jody."

"You tell my father you love me, but you won't tell me!"

"I don't hear you saying anything."

She took a deep breath. "All right, I love you, okay?"

"That's real romantic, Ariel."

"I said it, didn't I?"

Scott got up and headed for the house. "I need another drink, how about you?"

"I could use one."

He was gone several minutes, during which Ariel cursed her father's precipitous arrival. Things had been going along fine until he showed up to interfere. Now Scott was almost obliged to propose to her and the whole thing was embarrassing her to death.

But at least he'd finally admitted out loud that he loved her. He had even said he was crazy about the kids. Of course he could have been trying to soften up Red, but she didn't really think so. Scott wasn't the type to say something he didn't mean.

When Scott returned with the drinks, he motioned her to come sit beside him on the swing. "Let's talk about this like adults, okay?"

Which was provocation, but she decided he was right. Taking her seat beside him, she said, "Okay, start talking."

Scott put his arm around her and pulled her close. "Could you tell me nicely, just once, that you love me?"

"Right after I hear you tell me."

"You're being really childish, Ariel."

"That's because I'm around children all the time!"

He turned her face toward his and kissed her, and she felt her tight lips gradually relax until she was kissing him back and wondering how she had forgotten, even for a moment, how it was between them.

His lips pulled away and he held her gaze. "I love you, Ariel—truly I do."

"I love you, too."

"I think I may have loved you from the moment we met."

She sat silently, thinking about that.

"Did you hear me?"

"I heard you."

"Well?"

"Well, what?"

"How long have you loved me?"

"Not that long."

This time he was the one to fold his arms across his chest.

"That's not true anyway, Scott. You didn't fall in love with me when we met—it was purely physical, and you know it. It's only in retrospect that you're romanticizing it."

"Maybe you're right, but I loved you in Mexico."

"Before or after?"

"After."

She beamed at him. "Me too. At least I think so. But I wasn't admitting it to myself just yet."

"So what are we going to do, Ariel, please our parents and make it legal?"

"No way am I going to let my father coerce you into marrying me!"

"He's not, I swear. Listen, I'm not afraid of Red."

"Then why is it you all of a sudden propose the minute he gets back?"

"Because it's Labor Day."

"What's that got to do with it?"

"You told me I wouldn't be seeing much of you after this, so I figured..."

"You mean you were going to propose to me today, anyway?"

"I was thinking about it."

She jumped up from the seat, sending Scott swinging. "I don't believe you for a minute! If you were going to propose, you would have done it in bed."

"Well, maybe I figured we'd get back to bed again!"

"Did you really?"

"Look, Ariel, I don't know. I was thinking about it, but you never say anything when we make love. Even women who don't love you usually say they do at those moments."

"Well, I don't!"

"No kidding!"

She sat back down. "Okay, do it right."

"Do what right?"

"Ask me to marry you."

"You're liberated—you ask me!"

"Never!"

"Then it's a Mexican standoff."

This time she put her arms around him and pulled him close. His mouth was in a hard line when she kissed it, but soon things were back to normal and she was so engrossed in the kiss that at first she didn't see her father and the girls coming into view. When she finally did, she was about to say something, but she saw Red leading them back out of sight and heard Jody say as they left.

"Does this mean it's a happy ending?"

Epilogue

Rose had been right: They were perfect for each other, Ariel thought as she followed Scott out of the Rosarita Beach Hotel and down to the warm sand.

They had decided to honeymoon there for sentimental reasons, and the room was a vast improvement over the one they had shared in Tijuana—no bugs at all, and this time the lizards were mostly outdoors. It was the longest time they'd ever had alone to themselves and Red had told them to stay as long as they wanted, he'd watch the girls. At moments Ariel thought traitorously of staying forever.

Scott spread out the blanket he had brought from their room, and Ariel settled herself to comfortably face the sun. For the third day in a row she noted that she was the only woman on the beach with her top still on, and she thought to herself, Why not? It might be nice to have a tan clear down to her tiny bikini bottom. She reached to undo the tie at the back of her neck when Scott's hand swung out to stop her.

"What do you think you're doing?"

"Removing my top."

"Like hell you are!"

"You're the one who told me to the last time we were down here."

"Yeah, but we weren't married then."

"All the more reason to now. You've already seen me, so what's the difference."

"That doesn't mean I want every other guy on the beach to see you."

She couldn't help laughing at his serious tone. "I don't believe this. It would've been okay then, but now I'm not allowed? You're not my father, Scott." Once again she tried to undo her top, and this time he pinned her arm to the ground.

"Don't do it, Ariel!"

"I'm the only woman on the beach with my top on."

"And it's going to stay that way."

"I never knew you were so jealous," she said, settling down on her stomach, her head propped up to watch him.

"It's not a question of jealousy."

"Then what is it?"

"Would you like it if I took off my trunks?"

"Go ahead," she teased, "but you'll probably be arrested."

"You don't care if other women see me?"

"Why should I? I'm proud of you—I think you look terrific." Especially since he grew back his mustache and now looked his age once again.

"Just leave it on to humor me, okay? I know I'm old-fashioned this way, but I really don't want all those guys leering at you."

"They probably wouldn't even notice." Especially with one young woman built along Amazon proportions only a few yards farther down the beach.

With a sigh, he got to his feet. "Have you got some deep-seated need to expose yourself, Ariel?"

She laughed up at him. "Maybe I do."

"Fine, then we'll go back to the room and you can do it."

She sat up. "You serious?"

He reached down his hand, a big smile on his face. "Come on with me and see how serious I am."

She wasted no time in joining him.

Just what the woman on the go needs!

BOOKMATE

The perfect "mate" for all Harlequin paperbacks!

Holds paperbacks open for hands-free reading!

- TRAVELING
- VACATIONING
- AT WORK • IN BED
- COOKING • EATING
- STUDYING

Perfect size for all standard paperbacks, this wonderful invention makes reading a pure pleasure! Ingenious design holds paperback books OPEN and FLAT so even wind can't ruffle pages—leaves your hands free to do other things. Reinforced, wipe-clean vinyl-covered holder flexes to let you turn pages without undoing the strap...supports paperbacks so well, they have the strength of hardcovers!

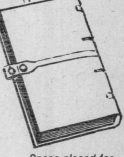

Snaps closed for easy carrying.

Available now. Send your name, address, and zip or postal code, along with a check or money order for just $4.99 + .75° for postage & handling (for a total of $5.74) payable to Harlequin Reader Service to:

Harlequin Reader Service

In the U.S.
2504 West Southern Avenue
Tempe, AZ 85282

In Canada
P.O. Box 2800, Postal Station A
5170 Yonge Street,
Willowdale, Ont. M2N 6J3

MATE-1H

Harlequin reaches
into the hearts and minds
of women across America
to bring you

Harlequin
American Romance™

YOURS FREE!

Enter a uniquely exciting new world with

Harlequin American Romance ™·

Harlequin American Romances are the first romances to explore today's love relationships. These compelling novels reach into the hearts and minds of women across America... probing the most intimate moments of romance, love and desire.

You'll follow romantic heroines and irresistible men as they boldly face confusing choices. Career first, love later? Love without marriage? Long-distance relationships? All the experiences that make love real are captured in the tender, loving pages of **Harlequin American Romances.**

What makes American women so different when it comes to love? Find out with **Harlequin American Romance!**

Send for your introductory FREE book now!

Get this book FREE!

Mail to:
Harlequin Reader Service

In the U.S.A.
2504 West Southern Avenue
Tempe, AZ 85282

In Canada
P.O. Box 2800, Postal Station A
5170 Yonge Street, Willowdale, Ont. M2N 6J3

YES! I want to be one of the first to discover **Harlequin American Romance.** Send me FREE and without obligation *Twice in a Lifetime.* If you do not hear from me after I have examined my FREE book, please send me the 4 new **Harlequin American Romances** each month as soon as they come off the presses. I understand that I will be billed only $2.25 for each book (total $9.00). There are no shipping or handling charges. There is no minimum number of books that I have to purchase. In fact, I may cancel this arrangement at any time. *Twice in a Lifetime* is mine to keep as a FREE gift, even if I do not buy any additional books.

154-BPA-NAWE

Name _____ (please print)

Address _____ Apt. no. _____

City _____ State/Prov. _____ Zip/Postal Code _____

Signature (If under 18, parent or guardian must sign.)

This offer is limited to one order per household and not valid to current Harlequin American Romance subscribers. We reserve the right to exercise discretion in granting membership. If price changes are necessary, you will be notified.

Offer expires March 31, 1985

AMR-SUB-3